"He will shoot you if you don't obey."

The hawk-faced Maurice kept the pistol steady on me through the open car window. He had a look I'd seen on other men: the gun was as essential a part of him as the hand that held it.

I held still while Traikov began running his big hands over me. "This doesn't have to get too serious," he said while he frisked me. "I figure you work for money. What you're working on now's earning it the hard way. Too hard. There's other jobs that'll pay you the same without getting you hurt. Or worse than hurt."

I nodded and let my shoulders sag. Then I swivelled back and drove my elbow up at his throat.

He got his own punch in. It struck me in the middle of my chest.

It wasn't as bad as getting hit by a truck. But it was near enough. . . .

GET OFF AT BABYLON

Marvin Albert

FAWCETT GOLD MEDAL • NEW YORK

This one is for
Joan Gabel
the loveliest attorney I know.

🔳 1 🔳

IT BEGAN WITH MY MEETING WITH BRUNO RAVIC THAT evening in May. His name meant nothing to me at the time. It wasn't until later that his tenuous connections to people I did know began to surface.

We didn't exactly meet. *Collide* describes it better.

I was at a table outside my favorite crêperie in Nice when it happened. It was in the section known as the Old Town: a dense jigsaw puzzle of aging stone buildings facing one another across short, twisty streets too narrow to have sidewalks. Seven of those Old Town streets converge on the Place Rossetti, a square fronting the seventeenth-century Cathedral of Sainte Réparate. The crêperie was on the corner of the one called the Rue du Vieux Pont. I was its first customer that evening.

The *place* and street were empty. The outdoor food and clothing stalls had closed for the day. Most of the quarter's restaurants were only beginning to open for dinner trade. The tiny sanitation car with its train of wheeled garbage bins had gone through, followed by the two-man team with the hose, leaving everything clean and damp. There was no other traffic. You don't get much of that in the Old Town. Few of its streets are wide enough for automobiles. Even in those, only one at a time can worm through. And if you don't know the neighborhood intimately, you find yourself having to back out of one dead end after another.

I sat at my outdoor table giving my taste buds a treat. My crêpe was a *Spéciale*: wrapped around a succulent mix of ham, mushrooms, eggs, and *crème fraiche*. I was eating it slowly, savoring each mouthful, when a girl came hurrying out of a seven-story apartment building four doors down the street from the crêperie.

1

She was small and slender, about eighteen. She wore dungarees with plaid patches on the knees, a much-scuffed leather field jacket several sizes too large for her, and suede boots. A canvas knapsack was slung over her left shoulder. She went past me into the *place*, moving as fast as she could without running.

I caught a glimpse of an uncommonly pretty, snub-nosed profile framed by thick, dark-brown hair that cascaded uncombed to her shoulders. She looked scared.

I wondered if it was before or after scared. Whether she was late for a date with a boyfriend or had just left him and expected trouble when she got home to her parents. Maybe it should have occured to me that she might be scared by something worse—but that's hindsight.

I watched her pop into a phone booth on the other side of the cathedral. The conversation was extremely brief. Then she was out of the booth and into the street next to it. This time she *was* running.

She vanished from my sight and out of my mind. I didn't know of any reason, at that point, to go on thinking about her.

I polished off my crêpe, drank the last of the extra-dry cider I'd ordered with it, and leaned back full of nothing but good mood.

It had been one of those balmy days the Côte d'Azur is famous for. The case I'd been working on had reached a satisfactory conclusion that afternoon, earning me a healthy bonus. I'd unwound with a long swim in the sea below my house on the coast near Monaco. After sunset the air had turned pleasantly cool. I'd put on a sleeveless lamb's wool sweater and a Levi's jacket over my open-necked shirt and denim slacks, changed from espadrilles into socks and sneakers, and driven into Nice feeling nicely relaxed. France was having its usual share of the world's troubles. But one of the sins and joys of being an expatriate American is that headlines about the stupidities of your host country's government don't raise your blood pressure too much.

I savored the moment, not letting past or future intrude. No nagging worries. No uneasy premonitions.

The waitress, a saucy twenty-year-old named Julienne Coppolani, came out to see how I was doing. She wore one of the customary Riviera youth costumes: skin-tight faded jeans, cowboy boots, and loose sweatshirt. This evening her sweatshirt had "BROADWAY" printed on it in red across her pointy, braless breasts. The last time I'd seen her she'd been wearing the one that said "HOLLY-WOOD."

She looked at my empty plate and said, in slow English, "You eat too swift."

"Too fast," I corrected her. She was in her third year at the University of Nice and worked evenings to pay her way. Sometimes, over those three years, I'd helped her with translations for her courses on English literature.

She nodded. "Too fast. You eat too fast. Do you want coffee now?"

"And a Breton *gaufre* with honey. Don't be stingy with the honey this time."

She stuck out a hip, braced her fist on it, and gave me a disapproving frown as she reverted to French. "You have a dinner date. You said you only wanted a snack to tide you over until then."

"Dinner's not for almost three hours, Julienne. If you want to mother someone, go get yourself pregnant."

That didn't faze her. "I'll get pregnant when I meet a man who deserves me. And you'll get fat if you eat so much. Be a shame, a man with a grand build like yours."

"I'm not getting any younger," I told her. "Eating well is one of the few pleasures left."

Julienne gave me the standard Mediterranean sign for "Who are you trying to fool?"—pulling her lower eyelid down with a fingertip. She sauntered back inside with a deliberately insolent twitch of her cute little derrière.

I smiled and relaxed some more.

Then a black four-door Renault maneuvered around a tight corner on the opposite side of the *place* and stopped beside the small fountain. The two men inside climbed out.

They were dressed alike: brown leather jackets and black jeans. Both in their mid-thirties. Brigade Criminelle inspectors with the Police Judiciare. One I knew slightly, the other well.

The shorter one with the strong, heavy figure was Yves Ricard, a tough, slow-moving detective who'd recently grown a short, pointy beard to make his round face look leaner.

His tall, wiry partner was Laurent Soumagnac, a neighbor and friend. He lived with his wife and daughter in Cap d'Ail, the village a few minutes from my house. Like me, he was only half French. The Oriental eyes and quick mind were from his Vietnamese mother. Another thing we had in common was Saigon. He'd been born there but remembered it only dimly, from his childhood during what the French had called their Indo-China War. I remembered it vividly from a couple periods of rest-and-recuperation during the Vietnam War. Same war, same place, same lessons unlearned.

Laurent and I had cemented our friendship over sporadic flipper competitions in our local bistros. Flipper is what they call pinball in France. French boys are passionate about it, and a lot of them remain so after graduating into an otherwise serious adult life. Almost every café and brasserie has at least one machine, and some have as many as five. All the machines were from America, which gave me an advantage. Laurent couldn't read the game instructions, printed in English. But he usually snuck around and played each newly installed machine long enough to get the hang of it before I showed up. So far we were about even.

He and Ricard crossed the *place* and entered the street where I sat. Laurent winked at me but said nothing as they went past my table. I watched them enter the building that the pretty girl with the knapsack had come hurrying out of.

Julienne brought out my *café noir* and dessert. There was an outrageous amount of honey on my *gaufre*. She set it down with a wicked grin. ''Go ahead and *get* fat. See if I care.'' She left me with another provocative swing of her butt.

I scraped most of the honey aside and went to work on the *gaufre*. Delicious. It was settling nicely inside me and I was finishing my coffee when Laurent ran out of the building four doors away.

He halted in the middle of the narrow street and looked both ways. He had his gun out but was holding it pointed up at the sky. Laurent had nightmares about shooting too quickly and killing someone by mistake. So far in his career he'd shot two men that I knew of. But very carefully: one in the leg, the other in the arm.

A man erupted from the next door down, wearing tight leather pants, his torso and feet bare. He was about thirty, broad in the chest and shoulders, his arms thickly muscled, his face rough-hewn and hot-tempered.

Laurent shouted at him to stop and surrender, starting to lower his gun but hesitating to take dead aim.

The other man brought his fist up from beside his thigh. It was a large fist, and it held a short-barreled revolver that neither I nor Laurent had seen until that instant.

He shot Laurent twice.

The impact of the bullets jolted him off his feet, twisted him around in mid-air, and sprawled him in the middle of the street. His hands clutched at his chest and stomach, his gun forgotten six feet away from him.

At that point I didn't see any more flipper battles in our future. More likely I'd be helping his wife and child get through his funeral.

The one who'd shot him leaped over Laurent and came sprinting in my direction. If he could make it across the *place* and into the maze of little streets on the other side, he had a good chance of disappearing.

I didn't have a gun. He did, and he was holding it ready to use against any interference as he neared me. I continued to sit there like any sensible citizen making a point of minding his own business. I kept my hands where he could see them, empty, on top of my table. When he came abreast of me I dumped the table over in his path.

His legs rammed into it and his forward momentum somersaulted him over it. He landed hard on his back. I landed on his midsection with both knees and all my weight. The air gushed out of him and his body shuddered. But he didn't drop the revolver.

I grabbed its barrel with my left hand, forced it away from me, and clubbed him across the ear with the side of my right fist. I had to hit him twice more before he went limp under me.

An instant later Yves Ricard burst out of the same building as the man I'd stopped. He took one look at Laurent and dashed to the black Renault to summon aid.

Laurent was unconscious when the ambulance sped off with him to the nearest hospital: St. Roch. The man who'd shot him was starting to come to when they locked him inside the back of a police van with his wrists and ankles shackled to a belt chain. It was Ricard who first told me his name: Bruno Ravic.

2

THE FRENCH RIVIERA HAS A NUMBER OF GLEAMING GLASS-and-stainless-steel hospitals where patients from the international set can recuperate or die in a reassuringly ultramodern ambience. St. Roch is not one of them. Its medical facilities and staff are excellent, but the place is very old and shows it. Interior walls are cracked and long overdue for fresh paint. The grime of generations of anxious footsteps is ground too deeply into the flooring tiles for any amount of scrubbing to get it out. The yellowish lighting gets soaked up by the walls and floors, making for a depressing dimness. It is not the best atmosphere in which to wait to find out if someone you care about is going to survive the night.

Laurent's wife, Domiti, got there shortly after I did. Laurent was still in the operating room with the surgeons, who were doing their best to keep him among the living. Domiti joined me in a small waiting room crowded with what looked like cast-off lawn furniture bought cheaply from a flea market. She was a short, plump woman of twenty-nine. Her normally cheerful round face was frozen with rigidly controlled fear.

We settled down together on a frayed wicker couch with battered floral print cushions. I kept my arm around her, and she finally relaxed a little and rested her head against my shoulder. After that we just stayed put and waited.

I hadn't been able to get to the hospital until I'd finished dictating my account of the shooting in Yves Ricard's office at the commissariat. He'd let me use his phone first to cancel my dinner date. Then he'd typed up my statement, I'd signed it, and he'd filled me in on the background.

Bruno Ravic was originally from Yugoslavia. He'd

slipped out when he was twenty, reached France and asked for asylum as a political refugee. That had been granted, along with a French residence card and work permit. For several years he'd worked in Paris as a waiter, but with ambitions to become a film actor. He'd gotten small parts in a few pictures. Not enough to support himself. Finally he'd moved down to the Côte d'Azur and continued to work as a waiter for a while.

Then he'd stopped working at that or anything else—though he'd managed to live pretty well on some unknown source of income. About six months back the police had begun to pick up hints that Bruno Ravic might be involved with large-scale drug smuggling but they hadn't been able to get any evidence against him. Nor even to determine what smuggling ring he might be attached to.

Last evening, while I'd been having my snack outside the crêperie, the Police Judiciare had received an anonymous phone tip. The caller sounded like a young woman. She'd said they could catch Bruno Ravic in his apartment with a cache of heroin if they moved quickly. The P.J. had assigned Laurent and Ricard to check out the tip.

According to Ricard, Bruno Ravic had sounded groggy when he had demanded to know who was knocking at his door. As though he'd been asleep. If so, he'd snapped out of it fast. They'd heard him run across his apartment and throw open a window on the airshaft. By the time they'd broken in he was out the window and heading up to the roof. All the roofs in the block were connected. Ricard had gone up after him. Laurent had run back down to trap him if he made it to the street though another building. The rest I knew.

Ricard agreed that the girl I'd seen hurrying from Bruno Ravic's building to the phone booth was likely to have been the tipster. But he didn't know any more than I did about who she could be or why she'd made the call.

It was almost midnight when one of the surgeons came into the room where Domiti and I were waiting. His news was encouraging. Laurent had been moved out of the operating theater to a recovery room and had a better-than-even chance. Shortly after that Domiti fell asleep against me. I eased her down on the couch and went to sit in a wicker chair with my legs up on the top of a wrought-iron coffee table. Within minutes I was asleep, too.

The doctor who woke us around 4 A.M. was actually smiling. "Your husband is doing remarkably well," he told Domiti. "His vital signs are all strong. If he continues to improve at this rate, we'll be able to take him off the critical list in a day or so."

Domiti took a couple of deep breaths before she got her voice under control. "Can I see him now?"

The doctor escorted her off to the recovery room. I was doing some stretching to get the kinks out of my back when Yves Ricard came in with a bag of fresh-baked croissants, two containers of coffee, and that morning's edition of *Nice-Matin*, the newspaper that covers all of the Riviera.

"Where's Domiti?"

"In with Laurent. Looks like he's going to stay with us."

Ricard smiled. "He's tougher than he looks."

I opened a container and burned my tongue taking a long swallow of coffee. While I wolfed down one of the croissants Ricard opened the paper to the third page.

"They had to go to press before we could give them much beyond the fact Laurent was shot by a suspected drug dealer named Ravic. So most of the story's about *you*. What they call your *heroic* bare-handed capture of the armed gangster. Makes you sound like Rambo."

I nodded modestly. "Just a typical American boy."

He gave me a sour look. "Should bring in a lot of new clients."

"Never hurts," I agreed. I bit into a second croissant and snagged the paper from Ricard to check whether they'd spelled my name right.

They had: "Pierre-Ange Sawyer, known in America as Peter Sawyer." It was nice they thought I was known.

Richard was right about the story romanticizing me: "American private detective in the tradition of Bogart, now operating in France." They made much of the fact that my French mother, Babette, currently a respected scholar in Paris, had been a Resistance hero in World War II. And that my American father had been killed helping to liberate France at the end of that war, four months before I was born. Also that I had been raised mostly in Chicago ("of Al Capone fame"), where my paternal grandfather had been a captain on the police force.

As usual, they'd gotten some of the facts wrong. The story made my father "Captain James Sawyer, pilot of a U.S. Air force bomber shot down over southern France." He'd been a sergeant, the bomber's tail gunner. The story also said I'd resigned from my job as a federal narcotics officer to become an investigator in Europe for the U.S. Senate and then quit because I'd wanted to go into business on my own. The truth was that I'd been fired from both jobs. But I couldn't object to that error. Made for a better image, businesswise.

I finished reading and said, "Nothing in here about that girl I saw."

"The reporter turned in the story before you told me about that. We checked Bruno Ravic's neighbors. They say he's had a young girl visiting him over him the last few weeks. Used to hear what sounded like violent fights between them. None of the neighbors know her name. Could be the girl you saw. But your description could fit a thousand other teenagers."

"There's those plaid patches on her dungarees. Thousands of girls don't wear those."

"Sure," Ricard said, "but none of the neighbors ever saw Ravic's girlfriend wearing anything like that."

"What does Ravic say about her?"

"That she's just some girl he picked up in a bar and he never got around to asking her name. Says the heroin we found in his apartment must have been left behind by *her*. Claims it doesn't belong to him, he never saw it."

"Not too likely."

"No. But he's sticking to it. A cool customer. He doesn't

act worried enough, considering the trouble he's in. That bothers me.''

"How much heroin did you find in his place?''

"Not much. One glassine bag of pure heroin, uncut. About an ounce. Less than twenty spoons. Plus a plastic envelope of quinine and a bag of mannite, for diluting the shit.''

Ricard scowled and shook his head. "That's another thing that bothers me. There's not a needle mark anywhere on Ravic's body, so he can't claim to be a user. Which means we've got him for possession with intent to sell. But he's never been arrested before. A first offense, for handling that small a quantity, he wouldn't have gotten more than a year. If that long.''

"Not enough to scare him into shooting a cop,'' I said. "That'll get him ten to fifteen years, even if Laurent doesn't die. A lot more if he does.''

"Against a maximum of a year if Ravic had just surrendered to us peacefully. It doesn't make sense.''

"Maybe he thought you had something bigger you were going to pin on him,'' I suggested.

"Like what?''

"I don't know.''

"I don't either,'' Ricard said. "And Ravic won't talk about it. Or about anything else. No matter how hard we squeeze him. He knows we can help get his sentence reduced if he cooperates and tells us about the drug operation, gives us his boss. But he just grins and keeps his mouth shut. Like I said, he's not as worried as he ought to be.''

"Ravic might be figuring on his boss getting him out.''

"After shooting Laurent? No way anyone'll get him out of that charge. I don't care how much leverage his boss can use.''

"I mean out of prison,'' I said. "Breaking him out. It's been done before.''

"It has,'' Ricard admitted, and he scowled some more over that thought.

When Domiti came back into the waiting room her round

cheeks were wet with tears, but she was smiling tiredly. Laurent had come to briefly and squeezed her hand. She was convinced it meant he wasn't going to die on her after all. We took her to have breakfast with us in a harbor café that opened early to serve commercial fishermen returning with their night's haul.

Dawn was spreading a rose-gold sheen across a flat sea undisturbed by the slightest breeze. You could see small clouds of seagulls wheeling above the incoming fishing boats long before the boats themselves came into view. After we'd eaten Domiti accepted Ricard's offer to stay at his apartment over the next few days. It was only seven blocks from the hospital.

It took me fifteen minutes to drive back to Cap D'Ail. I went up to Laurent and Domiti's apartment to check on their daughter, Charlotte. An elderly widow who lived across the hall from them had moved in to take care of the seven-year-old. She assured me she'd be pleased to stay with her a few days more. I kept Charlotte on my lap and talked with her until she was convinced her father would be well enough to be back with her before long. In the end she was more convinced of it than I was.

Then I drove to my house, a few minutes away.

It was on a steep wooded slope below the Lower Corniche. A solid old house my mother had inherited from her father. Thick stone walls and a Provençal roof of weathered orange tiles, surrounded by flowering bushes and fruit trees heavy with lemons and oranges. I plucked some of the ripened oranges and squeezed enough to fill a large glass. I drank it outside, standing under the gnarled branches of a big olive tree that shaded the brick patio overlooking the Mediterranean.

That tree had been growing there for over four hundred years. It radiated a permanence and continuity that was encouraging in times of stress.

The sun was climbing into a mauve sky. It was going to be another hot day. I was tired as hell. But I didn't want to got to bed with the poisons of that bad night in my brain and blood.

Finally I put on bathing trunks and went down the path and swam out into the cove. When I was a good distance beyond the cove I rolled over and floated on the long, heavy swells, tasting the salty tang of the sea, feeling the sun hot on my face and the undercurrents cold against my back.

From that far out you could see inland a long way past the shore cliffs with their fringes of palms and pines. All the way to the high peaks still glistening with the snows of the past winter.

I swam back to the little pebble beach and climbed up to the house and slept away the rest of the morning.

The next day Laurent was taken off St. Roch's danger list. By the day after that his condition had improved enough for the law to decide which charge to dump on Bruno Ravic: attempting to kill a cop—instead of succeeding in killing him.

Late the following night Bruno Ravic's attorney dropped in on me unexpectedly. I'd already gone to bed. Ravic's attorney climbed in with me and we became too preoccupied to discuss the case until breakfast.

3

"ACCORDING TO RAVIC, HE DIDN'T BELIEVE LAURENT Soumagnac and Yves Ricard were real police detectives. He thought they were killers sent by his political enemies to assassinate him."

"That's brilliant," I said dryly. "Ravic's an ex-waiter, a would-be actor, and a small-time dope dealer. Any one of those three would naturally generate an enormous amount of high-level political hatred."

"A little less sarcasm would be nice. If I'm to defend a client, I can't ignore his version of what happened."

"All right," I said, "*who* are his political enemies?"

"He won't tell me." Arlette Alfani frowned. "In fact, he hasn't told me much of anything. Nothing, really, except the bit I just told you. And then he seemed to regret even having said that much. When I tried to push him about it he told me to forget it."

"Ravic must be smarter than he looks. Realized how ridiculous it sounded. Better do what he said, Arlette. Forget it."

She shook her head. "It's the only possible line of defense he's given me so far. He didn't know Inspector Soumagnac was a *flic*. He thought he was shooting him in self-defense."

"Nobody's going to believe that," I told her. "Laurent shouted at him to stop and surrender. It was obvious he was trying to take him in without either of them getting hurt. He wasn't even pointing his gun at Ravic when Ravic shot him."

"So you say."

"That's the way it happened."

"You realize I'll have to do my best to break down that

statement when I cross-examine you," Arlette warned me. "I hope you'll forgive me if I get a little brutal with you there in court."

I smiled at her. "You were pretty brutal in bed last night, and I've found it in my heart to forgive that."

She actually blushed. It always amazed me that she could still do that.

We were having breakfast out on my patio. I'd put on jeans and a sweatshirt to go up to the village boulangerie for some fresh-baked *pain de seigle* while Arlette used my shower. She was wearing my old and rather threadbare terry cloth bathrobe, six sizes too big for her, and her hair was hidden inside the towel wrapped around her head. It didn't make her look any less sultry. That was her only problem as a professional lawyer.

Arlette Alfani was superb at both business law strategy and pretrial planning for criminal cases. But she still had trouble functioning effectively in court. She was too spectacular-looking. Even going without a trace of makeup and with her figure as concealed as she could manage under a loose-flowing attorney's robe. People had difficulty paying attention to what she said through the highly charged excitement of just watching her.

I could understand that. I'd been having something of the same difficulty since she'd been seventeen. Which made it more than ten years now. Of course, those years included a long hiatus during which she'd gone off to study law in Paris and then married a handsome Sicilian count. But the count had gone into shock when he realized Arlette intended to devote her education and near-genius I.Q. to something other than just keeping him amused. So now she was a divorced ex-countess, back on the Côte d'Azur as junior partner to the best husband-and-wife law team in southern France, Henri and Joelle Bonnet.

And back in my life. On a hit-or-miss basis. Arlette's round-the-clock dedication to establishing herself in her profession, and the unpredictable demands of mine, kept it from becoming a full-time affair. Maybe that contributed. Our get-togethers, when we chanced to be available at the same time, tended to develop into intensely erotic encounters. Arlette's carnal appetite was up there on a level with her I.Q., and when she turned it loose on me I couldn't have failed to respond in kind if I had tried. I sometimes doubted we could survive it full-time.

If there'd been nothing to prevent it that morning, we would almost surely have found ourselves back in the bedroom after breakfast. But I had a date in an hour with a *juge d'instruction*—the examining magistrate in charge of the Bruno Ravic case. Arlette was scheduled to be present when her client was interviewed by the same *juge* immediately after that. Neither of us cared much for quickies. Full-length symphonies were more our style. So we stayed out on the patio and talked until it was time for me to head for the Palais de Justice in Nice.

"I *know* Bruno Ravic can't be found innocent of the charge," Arlette said. "But it's my job to try to get his sentence cut down as much as possible. Extenuating circumstances is the only plea I can use. That he thought Soumagnac and Ricard were criminals attempting to trick and kill him. *If* he'll only give me enough information to make it believable."

I didn't say she didn't have much chance of pulling it off. She already knew the odds against it. I asked, "How did you wind up with Ravic for a client?"

"He claims he doesn't have any money to hire a lawyer. So the *Ordre des Avocats* had to appoint one to handle his defense from the rotating roster of available attorneys. It was the Bonnets' turn, so they got Ravic."

And they'd turned him over to Arlette. Naturally. Henri and Joelle Bonnet had come to depend on her brilliant behind-the-scenes planning of case strategy. But they had to reward her with cases she could take into court on her own from time to time. She needed that practical experience to work out her own effective courtroom tactics. Until she did, however, it was not surprising that most of the cases they let her carry all the way on her own were ones that didn't mean too much to them.

"Just don't put your heart into this one," I advised Arlette. "Ravic doesn't deserve it."

"*Anyone* charged with a crime deserves the best legal representation possible," she answered fiercely. "That's what *justice* is based on. The system of law can't operate responsibly without that. And without a responsible system of law, democracy is a sham."

Arlette's passion for the law was utterly real. It was probably her form of rebellion against the parental image. Her father had run a lot of the big rackets along the south coast of France. Though old Alfani had retired a few years back, other gangsters still worried he might change his mind and go back into business against them. That was why it was London he'd flown off to a couple days earlier, to undergo surgery for his ulcer. He suspected his old rivals in the underworld might be able to pressure French doctors to insure he didn't survive the operation.

"Did Ravic tell you anything about the girl I saw leave his building?" I asked Arlette. "The one who probably aimed the cops at him?"

"No. Nothing. Though I asked him about her, of course. As I said, so far he's refused to tell me much of anything. In spite of my explaining that I can't build any kind of defense for him without his cooperation. For some reason he seems confident that he'll be all right without any help from me. I can't understand his attitude."

I remembered Yves Ricard saying almost exactly the same thing. "Could be that he's been in contact with somebody else he's expecting help from."

"I'm the only one who's had contact with Ravic in prison," Arlette said. "He hasn't got any family to visit him, and nobody else is allowed to."

"There's the prison guards. Underpaid, like guards always are everywhere. Wouldn't take much in the way of bribes from somebody outside to get one of them to pass messages to and from Ravic."

"That's possible, of course," Arlette acknowledged

slowly. ''But if Ravic is trusting in that kind of help, he's a fool. He's in too deep for any of his underworld contacts to get him out of it.''

Yves Ricard had said something like *that*, too.

⊠ **4** ⊠

I WORE A BLUE GABARDINE SUIT FOR MY MEETING WITH the *juge d'instruction*. My shoes were polished, my shirt collar was buttoned, and I had on a soberly striped necktie instead of one of the less constricting silk scarves I usually wore to occasions calling for a certain amount of formality. I was not as impressed by the law as Arlette, but *juges d'instruction* are accustomed to respectful behavior. I usually give it to them. In my trade you have to deal with them fairly often, and they wield more power in a case than an American D.A., police captain, and chief magistrate combined.

This one was Madame Simone Cayrol. She was about thirty-five, a chunky woman in a lightweight pantsuit, with beautiful blue eyes under exquisitely curved black brows. Her office was on the third floor of the Palais de Justice. Its tall window looked down into the narrow Rue de Préfecture, between the rear of the building and the edge of the Old Town.

The steel bars outside Madame Cayrol's office window were new. They'd been added to all the second- and third-floor windows on that side of the Palais after a famous bank robber escaped from the office of another *juge d'instruction* a few years before. He'd jumped through the window to a ledge below, from there to the street, and vanished into the labyrinth of the Old Town. He still hadn't been recaptured.

Madame Cayrol's interrogation of me was little more than a required formality. She gave me a brisk handshake before settling behind her desk, with her back to a huge Air-Inter poster showing a jet winging over the Eiffel Tower. Opening her growing dossier on the Bruno Ravic case, she extracted my eyewitness statement and handed it to me. I sat across from her, read it, and confirmed that everything Inspector Ricard had typed over my signature was correct. Madame Cayrol asked for elaboration on several points, and a balding police stenographer seated to one side of the desk took down my answers. Another business-like handshake and I was out of her office.

If she appreciated my wearing a tie, she neglected to mention it.

I took it off and opened my shirt collar as I went down the steps of the building to the Place du Palais. Arlette was in the parking space out front, standing between my aging Peugeot and her glossy white Porsche, puffing on a Gauloise. She had a black briefcase tucked under her left arm and was wearing a linen business suit of a dull brownish color intended to make her inconspicuous. The skirt was modestly long, and he had several fountain pens sticking out of one breast pocket of her jacket and a small notebook protruding from the other. Her hair, which had flowed in sensuous waves to well below her shoulders before she got her law degree, was cropped extra short. None of it worked. Everyone who passed turned to look at her.

"That was fast," she said as I reached her.

"Madame Cayrol isn't much for idle chatter. You'll have a tough time getting her to swallow your extenuating circumstances plea."

"I'm hoping Bruno Ravic will be more forthcoming about that once he's faced with her." Arlette glanced at her watch. "The police should have brought him from the prison by now."

They showed up seconds later in a blue Renault police sedan. A P.J. commissaire I knew was in the front seat beside the driver. Bruno Ravic was in the back seat between Inspector Ricard and a uniformed *flic*. The police car swung around the *place*, angling toward the Rue de Préfecture, which led to the drive-in gate of the Palais. It didn't make it.

A small delivery van appeared from the Rue du Marché, which curved out of the Old Town and ended at the corner of the Rue de Préfecture. It stalled in front of the police car, blocking its way. The police driver leaned out his side window to yell at the man driving the van before he realized the van driver was wearing a ski mask.

I saw it at the same time. Arlette had started toward the Palais entrance. I grabbed her and yanked her back between our cars. In that instant a high-power rifle fired three times from inside the Rue du Marché.

One of the shots went through both rear windows of the police car and *spang*ed off the hood of a Mercedes parked behind Arlette's Porsche. Only one. The other two bullets entered the police car and didn't come out. I shoved Arlette down to the pavement with me. There was a lot of yelling but no further shots. Forcing Arlette to stay down by gripping the back of her neck with one hand, I peeked around the front of my Peugeot.

The uniformed cop, handcuffed to Bruno Ravic, had kicked open his side door and jumped out, falling beside the car. He had difficulty dragging Ravic after him. Ravic spilled out finally and sprawled on his back, not moving again. Blood pumped out of his face and throat.

Yves Ricard had gone out the other rear door and was crouched by it with his gun in both hands, aiming where the shots had come from in the Rue du Marché. But there were too many people crowded in there for him to fire. He shouted at them to drop flat. Some did. Most continued to stand there screaming. Ricard dodged into the street, shoving them aside in an effort to catch up with the fleeing marksman. His commissaire was on the run, too, with his own gun out, turning into an Old Town alley through which the van driver had disappeared.

Ricard and the commissaire were followed by cops flocking out of the Palais. Other *flics* were taking up stations around the *place*. I let Arlette get up, and we walked over to the stranded police car. The uniformed cop sitting beside it was cursing as he unlocked the cuffs attaching him to Bruno Ravic's corpse.

Arlette gazed down at the bloody, bullet-shattered face, her expression grim but not unnerved. She'd grown up with daddy in a world that had included too much sudden vio-

lence for her to go into shock over one more example of
it.

"There's one consolation," I told her. "You've lost your
client but not the case."

She gave me her Attila the Hun look and snarled, "Go
stuff yourself with nettles!" She turned on her heel and
marched away to where she'd dropped her briefcase.

The cop picked himself up off the ground and gazed after
Arlette with due respect for her temperament. "Your
wife?"

"No, just warm friends."

"Obviously."

Neither the marksman with the rifle nor the driver of the
van were found. Witnesses who'd seen the marksman were
no help. Like the van driver, he'd been wearing a ski mask.

Intensive police investigation failed to turn up the source
of the killing or pinpoint its motive. It also failed to prove
any messages had been passed illegally between the im-
prisoned Bruno Ravic and anyone outside. But Yves Ricard
and I agreed it was obvious. Ravic had sent a warning to
someone that he would talk if he wasn't freed. He'd gotten
back word that he should keep his mouth shut and he'd be
taken care of. He'd kept his mouth shut until they'd shut
it permanently. Someone had decided it was easier to ter-
minate him than to engineer his escape.

I didn't get a chance to discuss it with Arlette for some
time. She flew off to London that night. The doctors there
were worried that Marcel Alfani's system was too old to
handle the shock of having half his stomach cut out. Arlette
went to help her father decide whether to live out the rest
of his years as a semi-invalid or to take the chance of
coming through the operation successfully and being able
to live without pain.

There was no reason for her to hurry back. The Bruno
Ravic case had been the only urgent one on her agenda.
And that was over and done with. Or seemed to be.

The killing of Ravic in a police car in front of the Palais
de Justice got more news coverage than the shooting of

Laurent Soumagnac. National coverage, as well as in the local paper. The events leading up to Ravic's startling murder were recapitulated. This time the media carried my description of the girl I'd seen leaving Ravic's building. It was reported that the police were still searching for her, hoping she could supply them with some leads.

I already knew that. I also knew they hadn't been able to turn up a clue to her identity.

As it developed, I became the first one to find out who the girl was—three days after Ravic's murder.

⊠ 5 ⊠

HER FATHER WAS BROUGHT TO ME BY TWO OF MY CLOSEST friends: Crow and Nathalie.

"Crow" was what our squad in Nam had called Frank Crowley, and I still did. So did his wife, Nathalie, because that was how I'd first introduced him to her.

I was finishing an early lunch under the shade of an orange-and-green umbrella outside a Cap d'Ail café called Edmonds. They showed up just as Louis Bebelin left my table.

Bebelin was the manager of our village branch of the Banque Nationale de Paris, across the street. It was noon when he'd spotted me while closing the bank for the siesta break. He had come over to join me for a few minutes, ordering an *express* before sitting down.

"You saw Laurent Soumagnac this morning?"

I nodded. "They'll be letting him come home in a week or so. But he won't be doing any walking around for a while. It'll be at least six months before he's able to work again."

"At least he won't be in difficulty financially. He'll get full salary on disability leave. And there's his wife's income as a social worker."

Marie, the owner of the Edmonds, came out with Bebelin's *express*. Bebelin stirred two sugars into the little cup of strong black coffee. "Speaking of financial difficulties, Monsieur Sawyer, your checking account was overdrawn by almost two thousand francs as of yesterday afternoon."

"I deposited a big check in that account less than a week ago."

"That check was from a Frankfurt bank. You should

24

know by now it takes longer than that for a foreign check to clear.''

"I'll transfer some money from my savings this afternoon.''

"I've already done that for you,'' Bebelin informed me blandly. "I did it last evening. Before your overdraft got into the computer. Which would have forced me to make you pay a penalty. Just come over sometime in the next couple days and sign the transfer form I made out. To make it legal. So Paris doesn't start wondering what kind of games I'm playing.''

That's one of the comfortable aspects of small-town living. People know one another. Bebelin could take initiatives that would terrify big-city bankers because he knew all his depositors personally and could judge which ones he could depend on not to leave him holding the bag.

He looked at his watch and emptied his cup with one swallow before standing up. "My wife starts worrying about sexy depositors I might be entertaining in my office whenever I'm ten minutes late.''

He was reaching into his pocket when I said, "My treat. Call it a bribe for services secretly rendered.''

"Let's not call it that too loudly,'' he said, and he hiked up the hill to his apartment.

That's when I saw Crow and Nathalie cruise past slowly in his Citroën and turn into the village parking lot. Another car followed it: a classic Jaguar, superbly reconditioned. Its chassis was gorgeous, and the motor purred. I was too occupied in admiring the car to pay much attention to the man driving it.

Crow led the way from the parking lot to my table: a stocky redhead with a freckled, blunt-featured face set in its habitual expression of quizzical cool. As usual, his clothes were casual to the point of sloppiness. "You weren't home,'' he said as he dropped into a chair beside me, "so I figured you might be around here.''

Nathalie trailed behind, walking slowly with the driver of the Jag, speaking to him quietly about something that evidently troubled him. I'd known her a lot longer than

Crow. Since we'd both been kids. Back in the years when my grandparents used to send me from Chicago every summer to spend my school vacations with my mother at the Riviera house. Now Nathalie was chief of merchandising for the worldwide interests of her mother's fashion house. She was a slim, elegant woman, taller than Crow. But nowhere near as tall as the lean, wide-shouldered man with her.

Now that I wasn't distracted by his car, I recognized him. Egon Mulhausser. A former race car driver from Austria who had been living on the Côte d'Azur for the last two decades of his fifty years. He'd been one of the big stars of the Grand Prix circuit.

It wasn't age that had ended his career. The end had come after a spectacular crash on the Zandvoort track eight years before that had turned his Formula One car into a ball of fire. The face he had now, once seen, was impossible to forget. Plastic surgery had restored most of it, but the doctors hadn't been able to remove all the burn scars that had left him without eyebrows or eyelashes. Mulhausser had been a handsome man before the Zandvoort crash. He still was, once you got over just seeing the scars.

I stood up and kissed Nathalie. She made the introductions. "But you two have met before. My Christmas party two years ago?"

Mulhausser and I nodded that we remembered, though we'd barely gotten a chance to talk to each other at that party.

"Nathalie tells me you're a racing fan," he said.

"I saw you win at Monte Carlo," I told him. "The year you took the world championship."

"That was a good year," he said modestly. "I had the best car."

"You won some races where the car wasn't the best. Just the driver." It was truth, not flattery. He'd been a dynamite driver.

"Thank you. It's kind of you to say so." Egon Mulhausser's smile wasn't much. Partly because the scars and surgery restricted his facial mobility. But there was also a certain degree of stiff formality that was a basic part of his nature—and, at the moment, there was some worry he couldn't shake off.

We sat down with Crow, and I asked if they'd like something to eat or drink. Nathalie shook her head. "I think Egon will want to talk with you alone. Anyway, I'm due at my office in half an hour."

"And I," Crow said, "have a date to shoot a big wedding party in Nice." He grinned crookedly. "Most impressive assignment I've gotten in a couple weeks."

It was almost a year since Crow had begun trying to turn his photography hobby into a self-supporting career. Before that he'd been a prosperous computer programmer. First in California. Then with his own company in Nice, after he'd fallen for Nathalie while spending a holiday at my house and decided to become a fellow expatriate. But he'd gotten fed up with running a business and had sold his end of the company to his French partner last year and opened a photography studio. He hadn't made a big thing of doing so, nor of the fact that so far it hadn't paid off. That was Crow; he never made a big deal out of anything— on the surface.

Like in Nam, where they'd made him an antisniper sniper. He'd shrugged off his prowess at it; claiming it was due to nothing but sheer cowardice.

"You know *approximately* where the sniper is," he'd explained once. "And while you're moving into a position within range of him he gets to know *about* where you are. From then on it's just a matter of outwaiting each other. The first one to move again after that gives away his exact position—and gets shot. Well, I don't care how patient that other bastard is, he's going to be the first to move. Even if it takes a week. I'm not going to budge. Not even a finger to brush a fire ant from my eye. Because I'm too terrified to move. Just plain frozen scared."

Nathalie had seated herself with Mulhausser across the table from Crow and me. She looked inquiringly at Mulhausser and then back to me. "Egon needs a private investigator to help with a personal problem. He came to us because he knows you're my oldest friend.''

She put a reassuring hand on his muscular wrist while she spoke. Mulhausser's success with women, back when he'd been a Grand Prix star, had been notable even among other racing drivers, all of whom attract groupies the way a farm dog draws ticks. There'd been a time when Nathalie had been enamored of him. Before she'd married Crow. Perhaps it was because she was one of the few women Mulhausser hadn't had to ease out of his life that there'd been no residual bitterness between them. I knew that Nathalie and Crow sometimes dined in the restaurant Mulhausser and his wife had in Eze and occasionally had the Mulhaussers over to their home.

If there was any of their former affection in the way Nathalie's hand remained on Mulhausser's wrist, Crow appeared not to notice. He was looking at me. ''The real reason Egon came to *us* first was to find out how much he can trust you, Pete. I told him I'd trust you with my life—'' Crow paused just a fraction of a second and then added, with no particular intonation, ''If not with my wife.''

Nathalie was as good as her husband at registering undercurrents without appearing to. Her removal of her hand from Mulhausser's wrist was entirely casual. ''Egon thinks someone he cares about is in trouble,'' she told me. ''It *may* be trouble of a criminal nature. He's worried about whether you'd keep what you find out from the police.''

Crow cocked an eyebrow at me. ''I explained to him about a private eye being like a priest. Or a lawyer or doctor. Sworn to secrecy, privileged information, et cetera.''

''Not quite,'' I said. ''More like a journalist.'' I looked to Egon Mulhausser. ''The law doesn't *exempt* us from answering police questions. But a private detective who spills his clients' secrets won't attract many more clients. It's a matter of reputation—and staying in business.''

He had been studying me with those lashless, scarhedged eyes all this time. And he still was, trying to make up his mind. ''Nathalie tells me you are the one who saved

Crow from prison on that murder charge last year. And that you used some extremely unorthodox—perhaps even *illegal*—methods to do so.''

"Crow and I have been protecting each other's backs for quite a while," I told him. "Going back to some nasty situations in Vietnam. You're just a friend of a friend. So don't expect me to take that kind of chance for you. What you *can* count on is this: I'll listen to your problem. Everything you tell me stops with me, whether I take the job or not. If I do take it on, I'll do what I can to get the person you're worried about out of trouble. If the trouble eventually turns out to be something I don't want to get further involved in, I'll tell you and quit. But again, what I've learned won't be used in any way that might hurt you. Good enough?''

Egon Mulhausser studied me for another moment and nodded. "Good enough.''

Crow got to his feet and flipped a hand at me. "See you, buddy.''

Nathalie stood up, looking like she was going to kiss Mulhausser goodbye, but she didn't. Instead she patted his shoulder and then put an arm around Crow's waist and yanked him close to her as they went off to the parking lot.

When they were gone, Mulhausser glanced around us. There were people at the other sidewalk tables, too close for him. "Can we talk someplace more private? Your office or . . .''

"I don't have an office,'' I told him. "I use a phone and answering machine instead and work out of my home. A few minutes from here.''

He waited while I paid Marie for lunch. Then he got in his Jag and followed my Peugeot along the Lower Corniche and down the hairpin drive to the house.

I resisted a temptation to see if I could take those turns fast enough to make a world championship Grand Prix driver fall behind.

6

I LEFT MULHAUSSER ON THE PATIO WHILE I WENT INSIDE to fix us drinks. Scotch and water for him, orange juice for me. I'd had half a bottle of wine with my lunch, and I'd recently decided to cut down on afternoon liquor before I succumbed to the popular French ailment of *crise de foie*. I was half French, after all. A doctor I knew in Paris had a theory that liver attacks fill the same role in France that psychiatrists do in America.

Mulhausser was giving the exterior of the house some knowing study when I came out. "It's quite old, isn't it?"

"The walls are. Built there a couple centuries before my grandfather bought the place. The rest was a ruin. In the village it's still called that: *La Ruyne*. He had to put on a new roof and all the rest."

"It is in good condition."

My partner in Paris, old Fritz Donhoff, had taught me it's best to let a client find his own way to what's worrying him. I usually go along with it, up to a point. I said, "They had good workmen in my grandfather's time. And I try to keep up with maintenance and repairs."

"Yourself?"

"I like to work with my hands once in a while. It's a way of unwinding."

"For me, too." Mulhausser pointed to the roof. "You'll need to replace some of those tiles up there before long. Around the chimney."

"I know. I've been trying to find old used tiles that'll blend with the rest."

"They're tearing down an old hotel over near Menton. It has tiles like these, many of them still solid. I know

30

some of the men doing the demolition. I'm sure I can get you as many of those tiles as you wish."

"I'd appreciate it," I said, and I gave him a gentle nudge: "That automatically makes you a favored client."

He took a sip of his drink. I drank some of my orange juice.

"How much do you charge, Monsieur Sawyer?"

My rates varied, depending on whether the job was for a big business or somebody bloody rich—or someone to whom the kind of money you could carry in your wallet meant something. I knew that Mulhausser had a good income but wasn't rich. And he *was* a friend of a friend. Plus he'd promised me the kind of roof tiles that were increasingly hard to get.

I gave him a rate that took all of that into consideration. "Plus expenses, which mount up. And if I have to hire help, it could cost fees equal to mine for the days I use that help."

"I'm sure I can take care of it," he said. "Our restaurant is doing quite well lately, as you may have heard."

I had heard. The place was called La Grange. It had existed up there in the perched village of Eze for years without doing all that well—until it had been taken over by Mulhausser and his wife, Libby Arlen. Some years back she had been a sex symbol in Hollywood films, and then in France, where she'd been married for a time to a top director named Charles Jacquier. She'd drawn the movie crowd to their restaurant, while Mulhausser had pulled the luminaries of the sports world.

That in turn drew the kind of people who like to go where they might find themselves dining and drinking next to celebrities. La Grange was becoming a jet set favorite. I hadn't been there, although I'd been told it had a great chef and a pleasantly redone setting. I preferred restaurants where they just charged for a good meal, not for the privilege of watching famous faces eat.

Mulhausser took another sip of his scotch and water and asked, "Did you know I was married before?"

"No." I could feel it: He was getting down to why he needed me.

"Her name was Sabine. A French girl. It . . . was a painful marriage for her." Mulhausser hesitated, as though seeking the easiest way to tell something that had no easy way. "I should never have gotten married. To Sabine or anyone else. I was too young for marriage. Not in age, you understand. In the kind of man I was. There were too many women. Beautiful, passionate, treating me as though I were a god. And I had to have them all. I married Sabine, and I think I loved her—but I had to have *them*. That's what I mean by too young. I'm not like that now. But I was then."

He took a long swallow from his drink and set the glass down slowly on the patio table, looking at some point above and beyond me. From the direction of his gaze I guessed it was on the tiles around the chimney that needed replacing.

"One night when she was expecting me and I didn't come home, Sabine got in her car and drove out to look for me. It was raining. Perhaps a truck that had taken the road before her had spilled some oil. The car skidded and rammed against the side of a cliff. She was killed."

He fell silent, his gaze moving slowly along the top of my roof as though seeking more repair work that needed doing.

"When was this?" I asked him.

"Nine years ago."

"The year before you crashed in the Dutch Grand Prix."

"Yes." Mulhausser looked at me then. It was hard to read expressions on that face. "That was all I could think of when I felt my car slide out of control toward that barrier alongside the Zandvoort track. That *this* was how my wife had died. And that fate had waited a year to show me what it felt like to die that way."

He finished the last of his drink. I said, "Like a refill?"

He looked at his glass and was surprised to see it empty. "No. I don't have to get drunk to say these things."

"Sometimes it makes the words hurt less."

"They *should* hurt. If they don't, I am only an animal."

I waited.

"We had a daughter. Sabine and I. I still have her—a daughter. Though I have hardly seen her in nine years. Odile is her name. She blamed me for her mother's death. She refused to stay with me after that. Her aunt, Sabine's older sister, finally took Odile to live with her. Ines—she had no children of her own. Partly because she often suffered from ill health. Also, her husband was much older than she. He died the year before Odile moved in with Ines. Left her an ample income and a good apartment in Paris, as well as some country property. Even a small vacation studio not far from here. In Villefranche. Odile going to live with her aunt in Paris did seem the best solution, at the time."

Mulhausser picked up his empty glass and held it in one hand, looking at it. Like Hamlet with the skull of Yorick. "Odile was ten years old when her mother died. She is nineteen now. Nine years. For seven of those years I had no contact with her at all. When I tried to see her Odile would run away and hide. When I called her aunt's place in Paris Odile refused to come to the phone. When I sent her letters or presents—her aunt said Odile burned them.

"Then, two years ago, Ines died. She left everything to Odile. Her income had just about ended by then, but there was her property. Odile got that and a small savings account put aside for her education. But Odile was only seventeen then. Too young to be left to live alone."

He put aside the empty glass and looked at me. "As you know, I married again. A former screen actress. Libby Arlen. A wonderful woman, but almost my age. I won't have any other children. There's only Odile. My daughter. So I forced her to come down here to live with us."

He became silent again. Finally I said, "But it didn't work out."

"No. It didn't. Odile got along well enough with Libby. Everyone does. But Odile couldn't stand being near me. It made her act like a wild creature. She began running around with the kind of boys—and men—I couldn't approve of as her father. I tried to stop her. And she left. Went to live for a time in the studio in Villefranche that she'd inherited from her aunt. And then went back to Paris.

"What could I do? Get the police to drag her back because she was a minor? She would only have run off again. And soon she was no longer a minor. I learned that she had begun going to the College de France. I also learned that she no longer bore my name. She changed it. Took her mother's maiden name, Garnier. Odile Garnier. My daughter. I didn't see her again for two years."

He fell silent again. But this time he resumed without prompting. "Until one night last week. The same night that police detective was shot in Nice, by the man you caught. Bruno Ravic."

"Odile phoned me that night. From a public phone on the outskirts of Nice. I'd had no idea she was down here. She told me she was having a 'little trouble.' But when I asked what it was, she wouldn't tell me. All she would say was that she needed my help.

"She said she wanted to get back to Paris quickly. But she didn't want to take a plane or train, or hire a car. She wanted me to come pick her up and drive her to Paris. That night."

"Which you did."

"Yes." Mulhausser shrugged slightly. "I've never stopped wanting her to regard me as a real father, you see. Someone she could turn to . . . and finally she was giving me that chance. I *couldn't* refuse her.

"I drove most of the night. She wouldn't answer my questions, would hardly look at me. At one point I did have a feeling she *wanted* to tell me something. But I could have been wrong about that. She just sat beside me for about the first hour, very tense, staring ahead and saying nothing. Then she climbed into the back and slept through the rest of the drive. Or perhaps she was only pretending to sleep—so she wouldn't have to talk. I can't be sure.

"When we reached Paris, Odile wouldn't let me take

her to her apartment. She made me drop her off at a taxi stand. And that's the last I've seen of her.''

"You think your daughter's the girl I saw leave Bruno Ravic's building," I said. "The one who probably let the police know they could find him with heroin in his apartment.''

"Yes. I read your description of her a few days ago, after Ravic was killed. I think the girl was Odile.''

"My description wasn't much. It could fit so many others.''

"Odile was wearing a leather jacket too big for her when I picked her up outside Nice,'' Mulhausser told me. "She was carrying a knapsack. And she had on dungarees—with plaid patches on the knees. Exactly the way she was dressed in your description. There couldn't have been too many girls that age running around Nice dressed like that, with both a knapsack and those patches, on that particular night.''

"No,'' I admitted. "But that still doesn't make it *certain* it was your daughter I saw.''

"I *hope* it wasn't. That would be a relief. To learn Odile was telling the truth when she said she was in a *little* trouble. Not trouble involving dope dealers and killing. If that's what you find out, I'll be grateful. You'll have more than earned whatever I have to pay you.''

"Do you have a picture of your daughter?''

"No. I tried to take some of her when she was staying with us two years ago. But whenever I approached her with a camera she walked away. She couldn't tolerate my trying to act like a normal father.'' He sighed and rubbed the scar tissue covering one cheekbone with blunt fingertips. "It is not pleasant, having someone around who dislikes you that much.''

"My description of her was in the papers three days ago,'' I said. "Why did you wait until now?''

"The police are looking for her. I didn't want to take any risk of their finding out who she is. If it *is* Odile. I tried to find her myself. By phone first. I called her Paris apartment, but there was no answer. I tried the studio in

Villefranche, in case she'd come back down. I've continued to phone both places, but nobody ever answers. Finally I went back up to Paris. She's not at her apartment, and I couldn't find anyone who knows where she might be.''

"Any idea how long your daughter was down here, before you picked her up outside Nice that night?"

"I asked Odile that. She just said 'for a while'—and that's all I could get out of her."

"Was she using the Villefranche studio while she was here this time?"

"I assume she was. But I can't be sure." Mulhausser leaned toward me, resting his forearms on the wicker table, his strong hands clasped together. "I need your help to find my daughter, Monsieur Sawyer. If she *is* in trouble, I want you to help me get her out of it. Will you do it? Will you try to help me?"

I was remembering another parent who'd asked me that. Another daughter I'd tried to find and save from the trouble she'd gotten herself into. That had been more than a year ago, back in the previous April. I still got a heavy knot in the pit of my stomach when I thought about how that one had gone wrong—and about what I might have done differently to prevent it. Mulhausser's problem with his daughter had the makings of family tragedy like that one. I didn't want to get involved and risk failing to prevent this one. There were enough cases around that didn't stick you with a feeling of person-to-person responsibility that vital.

I drank the rest of my orange juice. I looked at Egon Mulhausser's burn-scarred face.

He looked straight back at me. Waiting.

I said, "Yes."

⊠ **7** ⊠

EGON MULHAUSSER COULDN'T GIVE ME MUCH HELP. He had the addresses and phone numbers for his daughter's Paris apartment and her studio in Villefranche. The country property inherited from her aunt—a small parcel of land without any dwelling—Odile had sold more than a year before. Mulhausser assumed she'd sold it to have more to live on while going through college.

He had checked at the College de France while in Paris. Odile Garnier was still registered as a student there. But she hadn't returned to any of her courses after the end of the Easter vacation the previous month.

He'd also had a banker friend check with the Paris bank where Odile kept her accounts. Her savings account had been depleted for almost four months. Her checking account had been canceled two months earlier because she's bounced too many checks. Which was another cause for her father to worry: "Odile *should* still have money left from the sale of the country property, and from her aunt's savings account."

He didn't know who any of her friends were. She didn't have any relatives left other than him. When she'd stayed with him two years ago she'd gone to discos and the beaches, and sometimes to museums. He had no idea of what her other interests were.

"And that's all I know about my daughter," Mulhausser said. "That doesn't make me much of a father, does it?"

"Not your fault."

"Yes it is. Odile was never able to forget that her mother died because of my irresponsibility."

"It was an accident. The kind that happens all the time.

Your first wife could have gotten killed exactly the same way going out to do some shopping.

"But she didn't. She got killed looking for me." Mulhausser glanced at his watch and stood up. "I have to get back to the restaurant. I left Libby to deal with the lunch crowd and the cleaning up. I want to help her prepare everything for the dinner trade. We're starting to be fully booked every day now."

That figured. May was the month that kicked off the Riviera's summer season, because it included two of the biggest events of the year. The first was the Film Festival in Cannes, already starting. After that there'd be the Monte Carlo Grand Prix. It was in May that all the tourist businesses along the Côte d'Azur really got rolling.

"You'll let me know," Mulhausser said, "as soon as you find out anything?"

I assured him I would.

When he was gone the first thing I did was to phone Fritz Donhoff in Paris. That was where Mulhausser had driven his daughter, and that was where she had her apartment and went to school. And this was Fritz's kind of case. He had spent much of his seventy-four years specializing in finding missing persons.

Fritz had been a police detective in Munich when the Nazi takeover had made it advisable to him to get out of his native country rather quickly. He'd settled in Paris and become part of the Resistance during the war. After the war Europe was full of people trying to find loved ones they'd lost. Fritz had discovered he was good at that kind of job, and it remained the kind he liked to do best, though there were other kinds of work that brought an investigator bigger financial rewards.

We had been partners for some years before I'd decided to settle in the south. I still owned an apartment next to his in Paris, and we continued to operate as partners whenever one of us needed the other's help. He didn't get around as fast as he once had, but he made up for that with what he could accomplish with a telephone. The vast number of contacts he had accumulated, during the war and over the four decades since, was the envy of the biggest detective agencies in Europe.

I gave Fritz the little I knew about Mulhausser's daughter and Bruno Ravic. I explained the importance of preventing anyone from connecting the girl we were hunting with the girl the cops in Nice were looking for.

I listened to his deep voice rumble its warning: "I'm afraid you are walking a shaky tightrope again, my boy. You could lose your license if they catch you at it one of these days."

"So could you, for helping me do it."

Fritz chuckled softly. "Yes, but at my age the danger is a therapeutic stimulant for the weary blood. Speaking of my age," he added, "I attended a gathering of other elderly Resistance chaps the other evening. In honor of General Geoffrey. Your mother was there."

General Geoffrey had been a lieutenant in the French Foreign Legion at the end of the war. He had led the capture of a considerable body of Hitler's forces in the Alpes Maritimes, which had saved the lives of a lot of Resistance members. He and my mother had both received their *Legion d'Honneur* from de Gaulle, in person.

"How *is* Babette?" I asked, like a dutiful son.

"As ever. Beautiful, sparkling, and girlish, with all the men fawning on her."

Babette had a tendency to act very girlish around men who'd already been adults when she was a teenage Resistance terror—in spite of the fact that she was bigger than most of them. My mother had a statuesque, athletic build that would make an earth goddess green with envy.

"She mentioned," Fritz said, "that she hasn't heard from you in some time."

"Did she mention she hasn't called me, either?"

"No. I didn't realize you two were in one of those stages again."

Relations between Babette and me were apt to be variable, seesawing between wary affection and armed truce. The problem this time was her husband. She'd married him after the war, while they were both students at the Sorbonne. That was long ago, but he and I had never managed to get beyond formal politeness with each other. Maybe if I'd gotten to know him better, earlier. But as a boy I'd spent most of each year with my father's parents in Chicago so Babette could concentrate on her studies.

Her husband had reacted to learning I'd become a cop with puzzled embarrassment. When I'd gone to work for the U.S. Senate he'd begun to feel there might be some hope for me after all. That hope had died when I got fired. A couple months back he'd suggested it was time for me to grow up and assume the responsibilities of an adult position in his shipping business. I had told him that most of the big businessmen I'd encountered acted as grown-up as toddlers trying to steal one another's toys.

I thought I'd said it with all due respect. He thought otherwise. Therefore, the present coolness between Babette and myself.

"Don't worry," Fritz told me, "you know your mother always forgets these things completely after a while. One of these days she'll be on the phone, wanting very much to see you."

"Fritz," I said, "mind your own business."

"Certainly." He let me hear one of his melodramatic and utterly phony sighs. "The way of the peacemaker was ever a thorny one."

We hung up at the same time. I figured his phone would stay hung up for about two seconds before he started using it to track down information on Odile Garnier and Bruno Ravic.

I stuck a small burglary kit in my pocket, locked up the house, and drove off to see what I could find inside Odile's studio in Villefranche.

Afternoon traffic was just congested enough to make it a twenty-minute drive. After passing through Beaulieu I tooled around the long bend in the Lower Corniche—with the brown cliffs bulging above the right side of the road— and there was the dark blue bay of Villefranche spread out below on my left. One of the largest and deepest inlets on

the Mediterranean. Crusader ships put in there for fresh
supplies and recruits. In the more recent past the entire
Mediterranean fleet of the U.S. Navy used to anchor in its
sheltered waters.

This afternoon there were only a French aircraft carrier
and a cruise ship in the bay. Little sailboats were practicing
figure eights around them.

I turned down off the corniche to the Citadel, the seventeenth-century fort that dominates the bay. The high walls
on one side were built straight up out of the water. On the
land side the first line of defense was a deep, wide moat—
now used as the town's largest parking lot. I left my Peugeot there and walked through the depths of the moat to
the fort's sea gate. There I took a sharp left and climbed
past the old pink customs house to the Rue Obscure. An
apt name: The cobbled passage tunnels underneath buildings on the lower slope of the town.

The address was near the end of the tunnel. I went into
a doorway and up flights of dim stairways in which the
smell of the sea fought the odors of rotting wood and damp
stone. Odile Garnier's door was the only one on the narrow
fourth-floor landing.

The little burglary kit I'd brought along wasn't needed.
When I knocked to make sure the studio was empty, the
door swung open. A small wad of cardboard fluttered to
the floor. It had been used to wedge the door shut when
previous visitors had left. They'd broken the lock getting
in.

I stepped inside and used the cardboard wedge to shut
the door firmly behind me. There was a single window
that looked out over the bay and let in plenty of sunshine.
The place wasn't big. A single room serving as living
room and sleeping quarters, a little bathroom, a cramped
kitchenette. A lower-middle-income studio. All of it had
been thoroughly ransacked by people who'd been in a
hurry to find something and hadn't cared how much damage they did.

The sofa bed and a studio couch against the opposite
wall had been slashed apart and gutted. So had pillows and

cushions. Their stuffing was all over the floor. Scattered among the stuffing were clothes yanked from the studio's single closet, the emptied contents of a suitcase and flight bag, things dumped from an overturned bookcase, drawers yanked out of a bureau that had been laid front-down so its back could be pried open.

In the kitchenette the floor was heaped with stuff removed from the cabinets and oven. In the bathroom the lid of the toilet tank had been removed so the searchers could rip open the float ball and tank ball. A hanging medicine cabinet had been thrown into the shower stall, but the smaller jars and boxes from it hadn't been opened. What they'd been looking for wasn't that little.

I spent over half an hour doing my own search through the mess in the studio. And found three items that hadn't been of interest to the previous searchers. They were to me.

They were among the things dumped out of the flight bag. First of all there were two Polaroid snapshots. The girl I'd seen leaving Bruno Ravic's building was in both of them.

In one she was standing beside a nice-looking boy of about twenty. He had his arm around her, holding her close. They were smiling at each other with what was obviously deep affection. Perhaps more than affection.

The other picture was a close shot of her alone, smiling at the camera and squinting against the sunlight.

The background of both pictures was a stone wall. There was nothing that told me where they had been taken. Not even whether it was city or country. Wherever it was, the weather had been cool but not cold: They were wearing padded jackets, but had them unzipped.

The other item was a plain postcard. It was addressed with a ballpoint pen to Odile Garnier—at her Villefranche studio. I read the postmark. It had been mailed from Paris on April 10.

On the other side of the card was a short message,

signed only with a tiny line drawing of a heart. The message read:

"Trog—

"Get off at Babylon."

8

THE DRIVE FROM VILLEFRANCHE UP TO EZE TOOK ME FIF-
teen minutes. Most of it was via a winding road that climbed
the slopes between small farms and clusters of villas—and
then skirted the vast Agnelli estate, a home away from home
for Italy's wealthiest family. After that I was onto the Moy-
enne Corniche with Eze coming into sight ahead.

If you didn't know it was there, you could miss seeing
it was a village. At a distance it just looked like rocky
outcroppings around the summit of a hill shaped like an
inverted ice cream cone. When you got closer you saw the
outcrops were houses built from the same brown stone as
the hill. All bunched close together with the sides of the
lowest ones forming parts of the defense wall.

There were three Riviera tour buses in the lower parking
lot when I swung off the corniche past it. Their passengers
were trudging up the steep slope to snap pictures of one of
the best preserved specimens of a fortified hilltop village
of the Middle Ages. I drove up to the highest parking area
and walked the rest of the way.

You couldn't get a car inside the old village. It had been
built so any attackers who got in found themselves in a
confusing series of death traps. Extremely narrow passages
climbed and descended and zigzagged sharply every few
yards. That slowed and divided the invaders while defend-
ers atop the buildings hemming them in rained stones and
arrows down on them.

I went through the rampart gateway, passing under its
murder hole. In days of yore that had been used to pour
boiling oil and powdered quicklime on unwelcome visitors.
Now it was choked with hanging weeds. I went along a
short passageway lined with little souvenir and antique

44

shops. When I turned into the next passage I got slowed by a traffic jam. A donkey in no hurry was ambling along ahead of me, with no way around it.

I didn't blame it for taking its time. It was lugging a big new refrigerator on its back. Donkeys are the only way the inhabitants of Eze can get anything heavy transported through the village to their houses. Hiring one costs more than renting a truck.

We soon parted company. The donkey zigged left into an alleyway. I zagged right up a flight of stone steps grooved by centuries of climbers, turned sharp left into another passage, and cut right down another flight of steps. La Grange was in a tunnel passage at the bottom.

The restaurant had been fashioned out of several connecting houses that were part of the section of rampart wall that overlooked the sea. The solid door was of polished oak, studded with ancient nail heads painted black. It was closed but not locked. I went in through a small arched entry foyer. Beyond that was a large bar and lounge. Its heavy wooden furniture and the tapestries hanging on its paneled walls were imitation medieval. But they blended well with the real stuff: the stone columns and vaulted ceiling. A doorway to the right led into the dining room, another to the left out to a patio with white-painted wrought-iron tables and chairs.

The young man behind the bar had his jacket off, the cuffs of his pleated powder-blue shirt turned up, and his black bow tie hanging undone. "I'm sorry, Monsieur," he said politely, "but we are closed until dinner time. That begins at seven, if you wish to reserve a table."

"I'm looking for Monsieur Mulhausser," I told him. "My name is Sawyer."

A woman was coming out of the restaurant section. She spoke to the barman in throaty, slightly accented French: "That's all right, Georges, I'll take care of Monsieur." To me she said in pure American, with a Midwest flavor: "Egon's told me about you. He's off doing some last-minute dinner shopping, but he should be back any minute."

I took my time looking at her. She was worth the time.

She was wearing a ruffled white peasant blouse, dark blue slacks, and an open cashmere cardigan of a lighter blue that matched her eyes. Nothing special. She didn't need to wear anything special. Libby Arlen made clothes look good, not the other way around.

"It's a pleasure to meet you, Madame Mulhausser," I told her.

She'd long ago learned to measure the exact degree of turn-on in a man's eyes. She dimpled and said, "That's always nice to hear. Especially from an attractive fella. But nobody calls me Madame Mulhausser. Libby Arlen. Better for business. The face and figure may be going, but the name's still holding up, thanks to those old movies on TV. Call me Libby. What do I call you? Pierre-Ange is ridiculous between a couple of Yanks. Peter or Pete?"

"Pete's good," I told her.

She held out her hand and let me hold onto it just a bit longer than necessary, giving me a gracious smile, a queen accustomed to homage but never bored by it.

"What'll you have to drink, Pete?"

"A *café noir*, if the machine's working."

She told the barman to bring it out to the patio, along with a *citron pressé* for her, and she took me out to one of the wrought-iron tables. The view from the patio of La Grange was spectacular. Fifteen hundred feet below, a Paris–Rome express was speeding along the track that followed the shoreline. It looked like one of those extra-small model trains people run under Christmas trees. Off to the west you could see beyond the airport on the other side of Nice, all the way to the Esterel Mountains. To the east you were looking into Italy, as far as San Remo. But even that view couldn't distract one's attention from Libby Arlen for long.

Her husband had said she was slightly younger than he, but that was old-world chivalry—or what some preferred to regard as outmoded male chauvanism. Going by the dates of the early Libby Arlen films, she had to be a couple years older than Mulhausser. There was a softening around the famous cheekbones and jawline, and her figure had gotten rounder. But she'd never belonged to the lean-and-hungry variety of sex symbols. When women's magazines ran those articles about how you and life could be beautiful after middle age, Libby Arlen's pictures were sure to be there along with those of Ursula Andress, Gina Lollobrigida, and Sophia Loren.

"Egon said he liked you," she told me. "And, of course, the Crowleys speak highly of you. I sure hope you can help, because Egon's pretty upset. Not that I blame him, with a daughter like Odile. Won't have anything to do with him and suddenly asks for his help because she's in trouble. But won't tell him what it's all about. Some daughter."

"Rebellious daughters are a problem you run into a lot in my line of work," I told her. "Parents don't get so worried about sons who go their own way. Figure it's part of their growing up. But when their daughters do the same it scares them."

"I wouldn't know. I don't have any sons. And my daughter, Chantal—she's never created problems. At least for me. Chantal lives with her father. I guess you know I was married to Charles Jacquier?"

I nodded. The young barman was bringing our orders out on a silver tray. When he went back inside Libby Arlen said, "It wasn't the hottest marriage. Except temper-wise." She seemed more amused than bitter about it. "We got married under a couple mistaken notions, you see. Charles thought he was getting a big American star to perk up international sales for his films. He didn't realize my star was already setting. And I grabbed *him* because I thought he could teach me to act. I was tired of being in Hollywood epics where all I did was wear tight clothes and pant at the camera. Charles had a rep for getting the best out of actors."

She laughed softly, remembering. "I've got to admit he didn't make me wear tight clothes too much. Usually I was stripped to the buff through half of each film he put me in. But before long I was getting too old for that. And too old to be an actress who couldn't really act." She drank from her glass and shrugged. "So we said goodbye and lots of luck. With mutual insincerity. Probably for the best, the way it turned out. Being married to Egon's a lot more pleasant, and running a restaurant's a lot easier on the ego and expectations."

Egon Mulhausser came out of the restaurant at that point. "Have you found out something already?" he asked me as he sat down with us.

"Maybe." I took out the two Polaroid snapshots. "Is this your daughter?"

Mulhausser put on reading glasses to study the photos. They looked incongruous on that face. "Yes," he said. "This is Odile."

"Then she *is* the girl I saw. And that means you're right to worry about the kind of trouble she's in."

His nod was grim. He'd been fairly sure of it before. But the confirmation made it worse. "Where did you get these pictures?"

"Your daughter's place in Villefranche."

"You broke in?"

"It wasn't difficult," I said, and I didn't elaborate on that. "The fellow with her in one of the pictures—do you know him?"

Mulhausser looked at that snapshot again. "No." He passed it to his wife, who shook her head. "But he looks nice," she said to Mulhausser. "Well-bred, intelligent face. If that's Odile's boyfriend, she isn't doing badly."

I took the postcard from my pocket and showed them the message written on it. "This mean anything to either of you?"

Mulhausser read it aloud: " 'Trog—Get off at Babylon.' "

Libby Arlen said, "It sounds like some kind of private joke."

Mulhausser told me, "Sorry, I have no idea what it means."

I thought I did. But there was no point in saying what I thought unless and until it led to something useful.

"Funny coincidence," Libby Arlen said to her husband. "Chantal called while you were out. *She* wants to find Odile, too. Chantal asked if we know where she is or how to get in touch with her."

Mulhausser looked puzzled. "Why?"

"Chantal just thought they might get together, if Odile was down here. Or planning to come down. Since Chantal will be in Cannes for another couple weeks, while Charles does his annual thing at the Film Festival there."

She looked to me. "Chantal still sticks pretty close to her father most of the time, though she's twenty now. It's sort of the reverse of the situation between Egon and *his* daughter. When I split with Charles Jacquier, Chantal was very definite about preferring to be with her father, not me."

"It's not the same as my problem with Odile," Mulhausser reminded her. "Chantal doesn't *hate* you. She just gets upset if people see the two of you together."

Libby Arlen looked at me with a rueful smile. "She just didn't grow up pretty, poor thing. Pretty isn't everything, of course. I've seen girls with strong personalities make prettier girls fade into the wallpaper. But Chantal isn't too strong a personality, either. I'm not the kind of mother she can be comfortable around."

"Can't blame her," Mulhausser said. "It's impossible for her to relax when she knows people are comparing the two of you and feeling sorry for her."

I asked them, "Are your daughters close friends?"

Libby Arlen answered me. "I don't think they've even seen each other more than a few times in all their lives."

Mulhausser nodded agreement and asked her, "So why does Chantal want to get in touch with her now?"

"She said they're relatives, in a way. And she just decided it was time to act like it. She wants to invite Odile to her wedding next month."

"Is she really going to go ahead with that marriage?" he asked disgustedly.

"Sure. Why not? After all, looks, charm and money— Tony Callega does have all three."

The last name made me sit up a little straighter.

"Though I do think," Libby Arlen went on, "that Chantal's letting herself in for more of her old problem, Marrying somebody who's prettier than her."

Mulhausser said quietly, "I didn't realize you were so taken with him."

"I'm not, darling, so don't get jealous." She picked up one of her husband's hands in both of hers. "You know my taste runs to men with that battered look, earned through a lot of tough experience."

Mulhausser touched his scarred face with his free hand. "Battered—that's a kind way of putting it."

"It's the face of a *man*, baby. Tony likes to *act* tough, but nobody would take the act seriously if it wasn't for his big brother."

"Tony Callega is garbage," Mulhausser said flatly. He turned to me. "Back when Odile was staying with us he dropped by one day and saw her. She was only seventeen at the time. He was already thirty. But he tried to make a pass at her. I caught him at it."

Libby Arlen grinned at the memory and told me, "Egon *threw* him out. Bodily. Tony looked stunned. He's not used to being treated that way."

"Maybe I overreacted," her husband admitted grudgingly. "But I just don't like him. I don't like what he comes from, and I don't like the kind of crowd he runs with. The spoiled types that've gotten bored with normal things their money can buy. Always looking for something crazy to inject new excitement into their lives."

I said, "This Tony Callega you're talking about. Any relation to *Fulvio* Callega?"

"*That's* Tony's older brother," Libby Arlen told me. "I see you know about him."

"A little." I sat silent again, chewing on what I knew.

Mulhausser told his wife, "I know *you* can't stop Chantal from marrying Tony, but her father could."

"My guess is he's *encouraging* it. Been almost four years since Charles has been able to get financing for a film. Now he's finally about to get one started. I'd give odds Fulvio Callega's his chief backer.''

"You make it sound like Jacquier is *selling* Chantal."

Libby Arlen raised her shoulders in a cynical shrug. "Well, there's no stigma attached to that—not here in good old-fashioned Europe. Downright traditional. Your practical marriage, arranged by the heads of the two families to unite their assets. Distinguished but broke aristocrat and grubby but rich merchant. The name Charles Jacquier does command respect in the cultural world, even if he's not exactly an aristocrat.''

And Fulvio Callega wasn't exactly a grubby merchant. A relative newcomer among the quasilegal heavyweights of Italy, he'd climbed fast and high. High enough to shuck the more conspicuous of the illegal activities through which he'd risen so fast. Nowadays he channeled most of his energies into manipulating legitimate big businesses and exerting behind-the-scenes leverage on Italian politics.

He'd made himself into a shadowy power, operating out of two main bases: a palazzo in Milan and a large villa just across the border between Ospedaletti and Bordighera.

A quiet spider, spinning barely visible, far-flung webs.

Rumor had it that one of those webs involved an illegal operation he hadn't dropped: major-league international traffic in dope and armaments. No proof of that had ever surfaced, however. A number of people who might have been able to supply some proof had died before they could get around to doing so.

I'd never heard of his kid brother before. "Where does this Tony Callega live?" I asked them.

"He's got a house in Cannes," Libby Arlen told me. "And an apartment up in Paris. Wanders back and forth between the two."

"Does his brother ever come out of Italy to visit him?"

Not that they knew of.

I left Egon Mulhausser and Libby Arlen and walked away from their restaurant putting together an intriguing line of connections:

Fulvio Callega was rumored to have a drug-smuggling ring among his activities, and had a reputation for silencing people who might pose a disturbance to his tranquility.

Bruno Ravic had been involved with a drug ring and had been caught and then silenced.

Odile Garnier had been involved with Bruno Ravic.

Odile Garnier's father, Egon Mulhausser, was married to Libby Arlen.

Libby Arlen was the mother of Chantal Jacquier.

Chantal Jacquier was about to marry Tony Callega, the kid brother of Fulvio Callega.

Chantal Jacquier's father was Charles Jacquier, whose comeback film was probably being financed by Fulvio Callega.

The line formed a circle.

A peculiar three-family circle.

9

"ODILE GARNIER HASN'T BEEN SEEN AROUND EITHER THE College de France or her apartment since her father drove her up to Paris," Fritz Donhoff told me when I phoned him from the tiny Eze post office at the foot of the hill.

"She isn't likely to show up anyplace that obvious," I said, "not if she's afraid somebody's after her."

"Her fear appears to be justified," Fritz said. "Her apartment was broken into four nights ago. A neighbor coming home late surprised a man leaving it. The man hid his face with his hand and rushed past down the stairs. In such a hurry he left the apartment door open. The neighbor saw the mess inside and phoned the police. They're calling it a burglary attempt, for lack of anything else. But it was obviously a search for something specific. Mattresses and cushions shredded, furniture broken."

The same as at the Villefranche studio.

I told Fritz what I'd found there—and what I thought about the postcard message.

"You may be right," he said. "Those people who get a sense of adventure out of exploring the subterranean passages of Paris *are* often referred to as troglodytes."

"Trogs or troglos for short. And most of them belong to groups. Very young people, generally."

"Yes. With an agreement to meet once a week, or once a month, to go underground together. A fixed time but a different place for each get-together."

"If Odile does belong to one of these groups, the postcard was notifying its members to meet at the Babylon Métro station: 'Get off at Babylon.' "

"I'll make inquiries," Fritz promised. "But it is going to be difficult. None of those groups have any sort of organization. Merely an informal arrangement among people who know one another."

On Bruno Ravic he already had some background information: According to the police, if Ravic had gone bad, it wasn't until after he'd left Paris. They had nothing at all against him up there. He'd established a good reputation as a waiter. Good enough so he could count on getting hired by another restaurant whenever he left one to act in a film.

"He only worked in three films," Fritz told me. "Small parts. He was introduced into that world by a fellow Yugoslav exile, Stefan Cikoja, a movie crew electrician. He's dead now. Somebody shot him a couple years ago. Probably agents from Yugoslavia. Cikoja was active in a secret organization of anti-Tito émigrés here in Paris."

"The Ustashi?"

"One of the smaller groups. The Matika."

"Was Bruno Ravic part of it, too?"

"Not according to what I've learned so far. That excuse he gave for shooting at the police—that he thought they were political enemies come to kill him—I'd say that was probably just a notion he took from what happened to his friend. It's always possible new information will prove me wrong, of course."

I doubted it. I told Fritz about the line of connections I'd just gotten from Egon Mulhausser and Libby Arlen. The line that formed a circle. That gave him new names to research: Fulvio Callega and his brother Tony, Charles Jacquier and his daughter Chantal.

"I admit some of the connections in that circle are a little loose," I said.

"Not as loose as you think," Fritz told me, and he paused to relish whatever it was he now knew and I didn't.

"Are you going to tell me," I growled, "or is this one of your days for testing my psychic powers?"

"Charles Jacquier. He used the same crew of technicians

for most of the pictures he made. Bruno Ravic's friend Cikoja was a regular in that crew.''

"The films Ravic acted in were for *Jacquier*?"

"All three of them."

I got back in my car and drove to Cannes, twenty-five miles west along the coast.

◈ **10** ◈

THERE WAS ONLY AN HOUR LEFT BEFORE SUNSET WHEN I reached Cannes.

I'd stopped at Crow's studio in Nice. Long enough for him to make fast black-and-white copies of Odiles's photo and enlargements of the face of the boy she was with in the other snapshot. I'd taken a few of each with me and left the others for Crow to messenger up to Fritz in Paris.

I parked above the Cannes railroad station and walked the remaining ten blocks to the hub of the action along the Croisette. With the film festival in full swing it would have taken three times as long to drive the same ten blocks. Every back street intersection was a traffic snarl. Down at the Croisette's divided boulevard the cars were jammed to a standstill in both directions between the beach and the palatial beachfront hotels.

But there was plenty of movement: thousands of people on foot, mobbing the six short blocks where everything important went on. I joined the crush.

It's never hard to find anybody who matters during the festival. They've come there from all over the world for the purpose of pushing their current films and working out deals for future ones. They can't do either by hiding. At the festival's information center they told me Charles Jacquier was staying at the Martinez. I also got a look at his photograph in an advertisement touting the film he was about to make.

At his hotel he'd left a message for all and sundry that he would return in an hour. He was attending the late-afternoon showing of a German movie competing for that year's awards.

I left the lobby and worked my way through the sidewalk

crowds toward the festival hall where the film was being shown. Across from it I managed to snag a tiny outside table at a brasserie called Le Harem. It was doing peak business. None of the waiters was likely to get around to me for at least half an hour. I sat back in my chair and watched the passing parade.

Casually dressed stars and filmmakers were striding from one appointment to the next, trailed by their hangers-on. Movie fans of all ages milled about, wearing everything from evening clothes to maximum exposure bikinis. Autograph hounds prowled for that year's big names. Flamboyant punks showed off their latest outfits and hairstyles, hoping some magazine photographer would find them worth snapping. Stoned teenagers stared blearily at the gigantic movie posters lining the Croisette while the noise and color flowed around them. Ragged child pickpockets drifted among the crowds. Young Riviera hoodlums leaned against the palm trees wearing expressions they'd learned from studying old Jean Gabin films on TV.

I didn't expect to spot Odile Garnier in that carnival, though it was always possible. By then she could have been anywhere. Still up in Paris, or back down here, or just about anyplace in France. She could also be as far away as Chicago or Singapore. But I didn't think she'd left the country. I had a hunch about that knapsack Odile had been carrying. If the hunch was right, she wouldn't risk carrying it through frontier controls.

But lacking a clue to her present whereabouts, the best preliminary procedure was the one you worked in most missing person cases. Learn as much as possible about Odile Garnier and the circumstances behind her disappearance. Try to find out what and who she was running from—and whom she might run to.

Fritz was handling the groundwork in Paris. My job at that early stage was to try it from the other end. Whatever trouble Odile had gotten herself into, it had boiled over down on the Côte d'Azur. That was also where most of the three-family circle she belonged to was centered.

And that was where Bruno Ravic had been killed. Which

had severed whatever relationship he'd had with Odile Garnier—and with Charles Jacquier.

That didn't make Jacquier the kind of hot lead that races your hunter's blood. Just a possibility. Coming to Cannes could prove to be a waste of time. But I had to start somewhere.

At the table next to mine two middle-aged men were arguing fiercely about a planned motion picture. The one who intended to produce it demanded six million dollars to let the other in on it. The other kept refusing to cough up that much unless he got exclusive rights to market the film in both Asia and South America.

A pack of news photographers went past and headed across the Croisette. They were escorting a nubile starlet in a red halter and silver hot pants. She whipped off the halter before they reached the beach, to insure a sufficient background audience for her sunset photo session. It worked. Even some of the small-fry desperadoes left their palm trees to go watch.

I got a surprise. A harried waiter arrived at my table. He leaned a hip against it, resting his weary legs for a moment. I gave him the moment and then ordered a croque madame and demi-bottle of rosé. As he trudged away someone I knew strutted into view: Sonia Galeazzo—better known to her victims as the Milanese Monster.

Sonia was short and wiry, with huge dark eyes in the face of a starving urchin. Her outfit was the usual one: old fishing cap, safari jacket, khaki pants, running shoes. The Nikon with its flash attachment and motor drive hung by a neckstrap against her chest. A spare Rolleflex was slung from one shoulder, a bulky photo-accessories bag from the other. Sonia was one of the most dreaded of the paparazzi, her nickname earned by her talent for catching celebrities at their worst—or provoking them to it.

She spotted me, glanced around to make sure there were no potential victims to go after, and sauntered over. I looked at what she had in tow. Sonia often used a living prop to help stimulate embarrassing situations for her camera. The Prop today had the look of a Playboy bunny. She

had a fresh, friendly, doll-like face. Her nipples poked out
through an open-weave fishnet blouse. Her denim shorts
had been scissored to show her naval and display ample
portions of her pert buttocks.

Sonia plumped herself down in the other chair at my
table. "Hi, Pete, what're you doing in this madhouse?"
Her English was as good as her native Italian. So was her
French and German. She used French on her prop: "Go
find yourself something to sit on, Murielle."

Murielle wandered inside the brassiere in search of a
vacant chair, oblivious to all the eyes fastened on her nipples and ass. I stopped watching her when Sonia asked
again what I was doing in Cannes.

"Broadening my cultural horizons," I told her.

"No, I mean it. Are you on anything I'd be interested
in?"

"I doubt it, Sonia. Just something I have to ask Charles
Jacquier about. He's across there in the theater, and I'm
waiting for the picture to end so I can talk to him."

"You're right, no interest." She couldn't sell pictures
of directors, producers, or anybody else who worked behind the camera. Photo editors only bought faces their
readers knew from TV and movie screens. "But you won't
have to wait until the film lets out," Sonia said. "Jacquier'll slip out before then. Nobody at the festival watches
all of any movie. Except the ones who made it and people
with nothing else to do."

Her eyes kept shifting while she spoke, taking in everybody in range, hunting for her next victim. Murielle came
back dragging a chair. She sat down with us and folded
her hands on her bare thighs, looking like a well-behaved
schoolchild waiting for orders.

"Do you know Tony Callega?" I asked Sonia.

"I've seen him around," she said indifferently. "Antonio—calls himself Antonio here in France. He's nobody.
Good looking, though."

"What's he do for a living?"

"I don't think he has to. All I've ever heard of him

working at is picking up girls. And he doesn't have to work too hard to do that."

"I guess he'll have to do a little less of that," I said. "Now that he's going to marry Jacquier's daughter."

"Is he? That's interesting. . . ." Sonia thought about it for a fraction of a second and changed her mind. "No it's not. Jacquier's daughter isn't anybody, either. Not even pretty." She focused again on the crowds.

"What do you know about Tony's big brother?" I asked her. "Fulvio Callega."

Sonia turned her head to give me her full attention. "Not a thing," she said evenly. "I spend too much time in Italy to know anything about Fulvio Callega."

"He that dangerous to talk about?"

"Who?"

"That's a surprise," I told her, "finding out there's somebody in the world you're afraid of."

"How can I be afraid of somebody I never even heard of?"

"Okay, forget it."

"You bet." Sonia looked around again. Her gaze rested for a moment on the two producers arguing millions at the next table. "Look at those poor guys," she said, lowering her voice. "It's been over ten years since anybody let either of them get in smelling distance of a movie. And every year they come down here to Cannes and pretend. Now they're down to pretending to each other. A guy without dough trying to con another guy without dough. It's a lousy business to get old in."

"So is yours," I said.

She gave me an elfin grin. "I'll never grow old. Somebody'll kill me before then."

I asked her, "Ever heard of Bruno Ravic?"

"No . . . Oh, sure, I read the name in the papers. That drug pusher or something that shot a cop in Nice and then got himself killed."

"That's all you know about him, what you read?"

"That's all."

"What about Odile Garnier?"

"Doesn't ring a bell."

"She used to be Odile Mulhausser."

That didn't mean anything to Sonia either. I showed her the snapshot of Odile alone, but she didn't recall ever having seen her. And Sonia was someone with a memory for faces.

She nodded toward the festival hall across the way. "What'd I tell you? There's Jacquier coming out now." Sonia stiffened suddenly, like a hungry tiger scenting a lone gazelle. "And *look* who's with him—Gillian Gale."

They were coming across the street in our general direction.

Charles Jacquier was in his mid-fifties, a lean, gray man with a sharp-featured, intellectual face. He was dressed in a charcoal-gray cardigan and black turtleneck shirt, designer jeans, and Gucci loafers.

Gillian Gale, the voluptuous red-haired actress walking beside him, had become an overnight sensation playing the major threat to a filthy-rich marriage in a new television series manufactured to compete with "Dallas" and "Dynasty." Which made her ripe for a star role in movies. She wore a blue silk dress that clung to her assets. Jade earrings set off the red of her hair, and high spike heels made her as tall as Jacquier.

There was another man with them: an athletic-looking, earnest type in his thirties wearing a neatly-tailored seersucker business suit and maroon necktie. I asked Sonia who he was.

"Gillian's P.R.," she said, but what little attention she'd given me up till then was gone. She fished an autograph book and pencil from her bag and gave them to Murielle. "Go to work," Sonia told her. "Gillian Gale, the redhead between the two men coming this way."

Murielle got up and went to work. Before Gillian Gale could pass our table with Jacquier and her press agent, Murielle was blocking her way, holding out the autograph book and pencil with a pleading smile. The actress blinked at Murielle's nipples but then automatically reached for the book and pencil. She hadn't been famous long enough to ignore adoring fans.

Murielle slipped inside Gillian Gale's reaching arms with the swift agility of a boxer and threw her the arms around the actress's neck, pressing bosom to bosom as she kissed her passionately on the mouth.

Sonia was on her feet with her Nikon, snapping away at full speed, shifting position to record the embrace from several angles.

Gillian Gale yanked herself free of Murielle. "You filthy pervert!" she screamed, and she swung a round-house at Muriell's pretty face.

Sonia's camera kept clicking, recording the punch and the ease with which Murielle dodged it.

Charles Jacquier stood there with a calm, sardonic smile. It wouldn't do his reputation any harm if some of the pictures showed him in Gillian Gale's company.

Her press agent made a belated grab at Murielle, and the next thing he knew his arms were full of her luscious seminudity, with Murielle smiling blissfully. Sonia shot that, too.

Gillian Gale registered Sonia and camera in that instant. "Get the *Monster*!" she shrieked at her press agent. "Smash her fucking camera!"

He shoved Murielle away, with some difficulty, and charged at Sonia, who turned and sprinted off up the side street. He raced after her but didn't have a chance. The three things any member of the paparazzi needs are to be quick with a camera, to have absolutely no conscience on the job, and to be fleet of foot. The Milanese Monster qualified on all three counts.

The press agent gave up the chase after half a block. By then Murielle had slipped inside the brasserie and out of sight. Probably to lock herself in the tiolet until Sonia came back for her. Jacquier had taken Gillian Gale's arm and led her down the Croisette, murmuring soothing words of reassurance to her. The press agent came back past my table, breathing hard, and hurried around the corner after them.

I stood up, left money for the snack that still hadn't arrived, and tailed them along the Croisette.

⊠ **11** ⊠

JACQUIER PARTED FROM GILLIAN GALE AND HER PRESS
agent in the lobby of the Martinez. They went into the
lounge for an interview with a journalist, the actress still
cursing under her breath and the press agent trying to calm
her down. Jacquier went to the desk and picked up his
messages. He read them, stuffed them in his pocket, and
strode back out to the Croisette.

I followed, not trying to catch up at first because there
was a chance he was going to a secret out-of-the-way meet
with someone who'd be of interest to me. He didn't. He
turned onto the terrace of the Carlton Hotel, speaking
briefly to people he knew at several of its tables before
settling down at a table bearing a "reserved" sign with his
name on it. If it hadn't been reserved for him, he wouldn't
have had a table. During film festivals the Carlton terrace
is *the* place to be. Every table that wasn't occupied had a
sign.

Nobody was waiting for Jacquier there. Whoever he was
waiting for, he was in plain sight of hundreds. No secret.
Not my kind of secret. Not even the movie industry type
of secret. I moved in on him as a waiter went off to get his
drink and the terrace lamps went on to defeat the gathering
dusk.

He looked up at me with a polite smile that said he didn't
know me but did know I wasn't anyone important in his
professional world or he *would* know. Polite, nevertheless.

I said, "Good evening, Monsieur Jacquier. Your former
wife, Libby Arlen, suggested I drop by to talk to you."

"Libby? My God, it's been almost a year since I've seen
her. How is she?"

"She was fine when I saw her."

"When was that?"

"This afternoon. At the restaurant in Eze."

"And she still looks marvelous, I'm sure. Incredible woman. Please—sit down, for a few minutes only, I'm afraid. I'm expecting some people on business."

As I sat down Jacquier said carefully, "If it's about working for me you've come, my new film won't even have a production schedule worked out for some months. So I haven't begun casting yet or—"

"I'm not in your business," I told him, and I gave him my card. One of the French ones with "Pierre-Ange Sawyer—*Agence Privée de Recherches*." I had another pack of cards that read "Peter Sawyer—Confidential Investigations." It was a matter of judgment, deciding which version to use. A lot of French people figured they were getting something more authentic if you let them know you were an American private eye. But Charles Jacquier didn't look that dumb. In fact, he looked damned intelligent.

He read the card, frowning a bit. Puzzled, not worried. "Are you working on something for Libby?"

"And her present husband. They're worried about his daughter, Odile. Odile Garnier, she calls herself now."

I was studying him while I spoke, but there wasn't a flicker of anything in his expression to set off alarms inside me.

"Does she?" Jacquier said, with a mixture of amusement and annoyance. "That girl has always been a worry, from everything I've heard of her. Refusing to live with her father, for example. What's her trouble now?"

"They haven't been able to locate her. She's not using her Paris apartment nor a small place she has in Villefranche. And she hasn't returned to school since Easter. No one seems to know where she's living at the moment. As I said, her father and stepmother are worried."

"I can certainly understand that. But—why did Libby send you to see *me*?"

"She thought you might know something that could help me find Odile."

Jacquier looked more puzzled. If it was an act, it was a solid performance.

"I don't understand why she thought that," he said. "I've never met Mulhausser's daughter. Not once in my life."

"I assumed you had some contact with her. At least through your daughter. She's been trying to get in touch with Odile."

Now he looked mildly surprised. "I didn't know Chantal had any sort of contact with Mulhausser's daughter. You could *ask* Chantal. She has a suite next to mine. Though I doubt she's there at the moment. Chantal is spending most of her time with her fiancé. He keeps a residence here in Cannes."

The waiter brought his drink. Jacquier signed the bill and told me, "I'm sorry I can't offer you something, but my business guests could arrive any moment." He started to hand me back my business card.

"Keep it," I told him. "If you happen to hear anything about Odile Garnier, I'd appreciate a call."

"All right." He looked at the card again before moving to put it in his pocket—and paused. "Sawyer—your name is familiar, somehow."

"It's been in the news recently. Involved with the arrest of a drug dealer in Nice, and with his subsequent murder while in police custody. A man named Bruno Ravic."

"Of course—*you're* the private detective who caught poor Bruno."

" 'Poor Bruno,' " I repeated. "You knew him?"

"Well, I was acquainted with him. Professionally. Back when he lived in Paris, he was trying to become an actor. I gave him roles in several of my pictures. Bit parts. He'd had no training, but he did have a good, strong face, and it came across on camera."

Jacquier sighed and shook his head sadly. "It's a shame, what happened to Bruno. I've been wondering if I'm not partly responsible."

"In what way?"

"Those roles I gave him. I had him playing young

gangsters. With that face and temperament, Bruno was perfect for it. I told him so. Perhaps that's why he finally decided to *become* a criminal."

"Ever see him again after he moved down here?"

"Once a year. I always come down for the festival. He always looked me up." Jacquier glanced at me curiously. "I don't understand—what has Bruno Ravic got to do with Mulhausser's daughter?"

"Nothing at all," I lied. "My involvement with Ravic was pure accident. Looking for the girl just happens to be a job I've been hired for since. No connection. But it turns out you can't help me trace the girl, so that's that. And since I did have a hand in Ravic's arrest, I'm naturally interested."

I watched Jacquier carefully to see if he knew it was a lie. But he seemed to accept my explanation.

"Of course. Well, the reason Bruno always came to see me at the festival was what you'd expect. He wanted another role in films. I had no idea he'd become a criminal. I assumed he was still working as a waiter. And each time I had to explain to him that I couldn't put him in a film because I wasn't making one."

Jacquier gave me a bitter smile. "You see, my last couple of pictures lost money. It's taken me years to find anyone willing to finance me in making another. But I suppose you know about that."

"No," I said. "I don't have much contact with the movie business."

"You're better off. It's a heartless business run by stupid people. A couple of failures and suddenly everybody regards you as a permanent has-been. People who used to fawn on you won't even answer your phone calls. They don't believe you can ever come back."

"Could make you pretty cynical."

"Oh, I've been that for a long time. I learned very early in my career." Jacquier looked at his watch and then toward the Croisette. Failing to see the people he expected, he went on. "Funny story. It was when I was making my first picture, with very little funding. My agent took me to lunch with a banker who sometimes backs films. I told the banker about my years of being broke and my struggle to get started. After the lunch my agent begged me never to tell anybody *that* again. About having been broke.''

Jacquier's laugh wasn't too humorous. "I pointed out that *everybody* has been broke at one time or other. He said that was true, but nobody ever mentioned it. In the film business it's considered a contagious disease—*ever* having been broke. Like saying you've had AIDS. People avoid you.''

At that point Jacquier spotted a newcomer arriving on the Carlton terrace and immediately dressed his face in a charming smile.

The newcomer was one of the top comedians of French films and television: Pascal Guillot. A fat man with a bald head and bulging eyes that stared at the world with a permanent professional incomprehension. He was followed by a small retinue: three gofers and one of the Riviera's highest-priced call girls.

Guillot paused at our table to grab Jacquier's extended hand in both of his own. The Hollywood handshake, now used by movie people the world over: proof of sincere affection, bestowed on business associates, strangers, and professional enemies with equal fervor.

"Charles!'' he gushed. "Congratulations on your new picture.''

"I haven't started it yet,'' Jacquier said, keeping his smile warm, "but thank you anyway.''

"With *you* doing it, it's a sure hit. I've been telling everybody.''

"I'll try not to disappoint you, Pascal.''

"You won't. You're a genius, Charles. The best.''

They beamed at each other some more. Then Pascal Guillot lumbered off with his retinue to pump a few more hands before disappearing inside the hotel.

"See what I mean?'' Jacquier muttered darkly. "I put him in his first picture, gave him his real start. For the last three years he's been acting as though he had trouble recognizing me. Now that I'm back in action I'm his genius pal again.''

A couple of other newcomers appeared on the terrace. Jacquier regarded their approach with a poker face that betrayed neither warmth nor hostility.

Both men were in their early thirties, and they shared an emotional deficiency you came to recognize immediately in my trade because you saw so much of it. An utter indifference to other people's pain.

One had a lean, strong figure in a beautifully tailored silk suit, with his cream shirt unbuttoned to show a heavy gold chain dangling across the well-tanned skin of his hairless chest. He had the darkly handsome face of a Renaissance princeling, flawed by a too-thin mouth compensated for with a neatly barbered mustache. He also had the eyes of a man who wouldn't take two steps to pull a drowning puppy out of a pond.

The guy with him looked like the one who threw the puppy in there. He had the build of a pro fullback: a massive bruiser with a dangerous blend of brutality and cleverness in his meaty face. His hands were extra-large, with flattened knuckles. His denim jacket was open over a body shirt bulging with thick muscle layered like armor over his heavy bone structure.

They parted at Jacquier's table. The bruiser walked on into the bar, light on his feet for a man that size. The handsome one offered me both hands and a smile full of perfect teeth that glittered with reflected lamplight under the mustache. I let him squeeze my hand between his.

''Wonderful to meet you,'' he told me. ''I'm Antoine Callega, Charlie's co-producer.''

I had news for Libby Arlen. She'd won her bet about where Jacquier's financing was coming from. But Fulvio Callega wasn't doing it just to add a touch of class to his family name. He was also using it as a way to add a move into the film business to his other ''legitimate'' interests.

''No, you're not,'' Jacquier told Tony Callega crisply. ''Your title is *associate* producer.''

''Same thing.''

"Not quite. And you can stop impressing Monsieur Sawyer. He's not in the business."

Tony Callega dropped my hand and his smile. He stood there and frowned down at Jacquier. "You mean neither of those distributors has shown up?"

"They will, don't worry. Where's Chantal? I thought she was with you."

"I dropped her off at the Martinez." Tony Callega settled into a chair. "She needs a couple of hours to make herself look good for the dinner tonight." There wasn't a hint of affection in his tone when speaking of his bride-to-be.

Jacquier told him, "Monsieur Sawyer is the private detective who caught Bruno."

Tony Callega shot me a brief, wary look. Then he said indifferently, "Is that so?"

I asked him, "Did *you* know Bruno Ravic?"

He hesitated. Jacquier answered for him. "Bruno was the one who introduced Tony to me."

"That's right," Tony Callega said. His voice was still indifferent, but he was having to work at it.

The trip to Cannes hadn't been a waste of time after all.

◧ **12** ◧

"HOW WELL DID YOU KNOW RAVIC?" I ASKED TONY CAL-lega.

"I didn't really *know* him. He was a waiter in a restaurant I used to go to for a while, that's as much as we knew each other."

"Is that where he introduced the two of you?"

Jacquier answered, "No, that was here in Cannes, at the last film festival. I was buying Bruno a drink and explaining why I still couldn't hire him as an actor. Tony happened to pass by, and Bruno recognized him. So he introduced us."

"Looks like that turned out to be a lucky chance meeting, for both of you."

Tony Callega looked at me with narrowed eyes, his thin mouth getting thinner. I figured it was supposed to be his dangerous stare. "Why are *you* so interested?"

"Just curious," I said. I gave it a second's thought and took a swing. "What I'm really interested in is Egon Mulhausser's daughter. Odile. She's missing, and I'm trying to find her. I understand you know her pretty well."

I'd just decided: If *he* knew about a connection between Odile Garnier and Bruno Ravic, I didn't mind him realizing that I knew it, too. I wanted to scc how he handled it, and whether it provoked him into making any interesting moves afterward.

Jacquier was saying to Tony Callega, "I wasn't aware you were friendly with Mulhausser's daughter."

"I'm not, not the way you mean. She's just a girl I run into now and then, just to say hello to. I haven't seen her in almost six months."

71

It was already paying off. I asked him, "Where was that—where you saw her last?"

He shrugged. "A bar in Paris. We said hello, had a drink, said goodbye. Why?" He was giving me his dangerous look again.

"It would help me if you knew some of the places she goes to, or who her friends are."

"Sorry," he snapped. "I've got no idea."

"What bar was it you met her in, that time?"

"Just one of the bars in Paris. Around St. Germain. I go to a lot of them, I don't even remember which one this was."

"You're not much help," I told him.

But I had a feeling he was going to be, one way or another.

Jacquier nodded toward the Croisette and told Tony Callega; "Here they come now." He got his professional smile ready as he told me; "You'll have to excuse us."

"Sure." I stood up as the film distributors came across the terrace from the sidewalk: a pair of heavyset men in dark suits. Tony surged to his feet, giving them the Hollywood handshake and saying, "Wonderful to meet you, I'm Antoine Callega, Charlie's co-producer."

I went back along the Croisette to the Martinez.

Chantal Jacquier was in the hotel's beauty parlor getting her hair restyled. I left word for her and went into the lounge off the Art Deco lobby. Tried the same order: croque madame and rosé. This time it came promptly. I'd had my snack and was refilling my glass with the last of the wine when Jacquier's daughter appeared, wearing her brand-new hairdo and a flower-print blouse with a peasant skirt. She glanced around the lounge uncertainly and then asked the barman for me.

He pointed, and I stood up and went to meet her.

She was tall and slim, with small features and a healthy, youthful complexion. She didn't have her mother's looks, but few women got to be screen stars in spite of minimal acting talent. Libby Arlen was a freak of nature. Her daughter wasn't: just a normal-looking young woman.

The only thing I found unattractive about her was the lack of self-assurance in her expression, and an accompanying defensiveness. It looked like a chronic affliction.

Maybe she'd overheard too many people say "poor Chantal"—too often and too young.

I complimented her on the way her hair looked and asked if I could buy her a drink.

"No," she said hesitantly, "I really don't have much time. I have to get ready for a dinner appointment and—"

"I know," I said. "Tony told me."

She brightened a bit. "Oh, you're a friend of Tony's?"

"I just left him and your father. At the Carlton terrace, getting involved with those distributors."

She relaxed another notch. "They're the ones we're having dinner with. We're all supposed to meet at Tony's house tonight."

"That's right," I said. "But that leaves you enough time. Are you sure you won't have just one drink? A quick one?"

"Well . . ."

I took her elbow and steered her to my booth, sat her down, and signaled a waiter. Chantal Jacquier ordered a scotch on the rocks. I stayed with my last half glass of wine.

She glanced at the back of the card I'd left for her. "Your message says my mother asked you to come see me. She didn't mention anything about that when I phoned her earlier today."

"It's because of your call that I'm here." I paused when her drink arrived. She took a healthy swallow. I said, "Your mother and her husband are worried about Odile. As she told you, *they* don't know where she is. They've hired me to locate her, and I hope you can help me with it."

"I don't see how. That's why I called Mama, to find Odile. So obviously *I* don't know where she is either."

"That's so, but it would help if you could tell me who

some of her current friends are. Places she hangs out, people she might be staying with.''

Chantal downed more of her scotch. Liquor seemed to
stoke her confidence a bit. ''I haven't the faintest idea about
any of that. Odile and I have never had much to do with
each other. The last time I saw her must have been more
than a year ago. And that was just running into each other
by chance. In a Paris department store. And then all we
did was talk for a minute or so. Just 'How are you' and
that sort of thing. So you see, I really don't know anything
that would help you.''

''That's a disappointment,'' I said, frowning. ''I naturally assumed, since you wanted to invite her to your wedding, that you and she were closer than that.''

''No. Tony just thought we should ask Odile if she'd
like to attend. When I called her apartment and didn't get
an answer, he suggested I find out if Mama and Odile's
father knew where she was. That's all.''

I didn't let her see what that piece of information did to
me. ''I didn't realize Tony knew Odile that well.''

''He doesn't. He just thought since she is part of my
family, in a way . . . and, of course, he's right.'' When
she spoke of her fiancé, Chantal Jacquier's manner became
an uneasy mix of pride and nervousness. ''As a matter of
fact,'' she added, ''I don't think Tony's even ever met
Odile.''

I didn't get anything else of interest out of her. But what
she'd given me was enough.

Tony Callega was trying to find Odile Garnier, too.

Put that together with the fact that he was tied somehow
to Bruno Ravic, and Tony became my first tangible lead.
One worth following for a while, to see what it—and he—
led to.

◪ **13** ◪

It was dark out when I walked back to the Carlton. The night crowds were as thick as ever, moving in and out of illuminated pockets under the Croisette's street lamps. Two of the big yachts in the Cannes marina were starting to shoot off red and yellow fireworks.

Jacquier and Tony Callega were still in conference with the two distributors on the Carlton terrace. I continued along the sidewalk past it, heading toward the hotel's lobby entrance.

An ambulance had fought its way through the traffic and pulled into the curved entrance driveway. Its revolving blue lights flashed across glossy green palm leaves and the milk-white facade of the hotel.

A producer had suffered a massive coronary while hosting a publicity bash for his latest film in one of the Carlton's private dining rooms. He was being carried out across the lobby on the stretcher when I entered. Few of the movie people packing the lobby interrupted their business conversations to watch him go. He was one of the movers and shakers of their world—but that was five minutes ago.

I walked through the narrow side lobby, past the temporary booths set up to promote some of the hotter films, and entered the lounge end of the bar. Most of the leather-padded booths were taken, but not all. It wasn't as important to be seen inside the bar and its offshoots as out on the filled-to-capacity terrace. I settled into a booth that gave me a view through the window-wall of Jacquier's table outside.

At the other end of the lounge, the bruiser who'd arrived with Tony Callega was seated at the bar. His stool was turned so he could lean against its padded back and keep an eye on the terrace. If he noticed me, he didn't show it.

I ordered a cappuccino from a passing waiter and kept my watch on Tony Callega. The cappuccino arrived as France's top pop singer, Serge Yonnet, came up onto the terrace. The famous grin flashed right and left as he strolled in the direction of the bar. His progress was delayed a number of times by people getting up from their tables to shake his hand, hug him, kiss him.

Yonnet didn't have his customary entourage with him. Just a rangy, wide-shouldered man with a crewcut and thick glasses. Jean-Marie Reju.

I knew Reju could dress with elegance when one of his personal protection jobs required it. This was not one of those occasions. But even at the Cannes film festival, where people wore all sorts of outfits, his raincoat was conspicuous. Few people use raincoats on the Riviera even when it's raining.

He wore it unbuttoned, as always. Reju favored unbuttoned raincoats because they provided both excellent concealment and swift access to the big Colt .45 he used when working.

It's not easy to get a permit to carry a concealed weapon around with you in France. You have to fill out a lot of forms explaining exactly why you need it and for exactly how long. Then they take their time considering your application—sometimes longer than the job you need it for. Jean-Marie Reju never had that problem. He'd been with the government before going private: part of the V.O. service guarding traveling officials. High officials continued to call on his private services. As in every trade, knowing the right people cuts through the red tape.

Reju followed his present client, Serge Yonnet, into the bar. Yonnet came into the lounge section. Reju stopped beside the bar, exchanged expressionless nods with the bruiser on the stool, and did a careful scan of everybody in the place.

He was a big man; as big as me. But next to the guy on

the bar stool, he didn't seem big. The bruiser looked like he could throw Reju over a roof without breathing hard.

Serge Yonnet plunked himself down in a booth occupied by a plump, pretty woman about his age who was gazing gloomily at the tall drink she held in both hands. Her somber expression didn't change with his arrival. I recognized her then, from a photo layout in *Paris-Match* of the happy couple at home. Yonnet's wife. The couple wasn't a happy one at the moment. They launched a low-voiced argument. They took a two-second break for the waiter who scurried over to take his drink order and then resumed.

Jean-Marie Reju came from the bar to my booth and said, "Shift."

I shifted to one side of the booth so he could sit where he could watch both approaches to his client's booth: from the terrace and from the hotel lobby. He hadn't given me a smile of greeting; but then Reju seldom smiled. I'd never seen him laugh. A humorless man. Which led some to regard him as stupid, as well. But I'd never heard of him making a mistake on a job. And I'd watched him play chess with Fritz Donhoff. Fritz was a strong player. Reju was better.

"Is Yonnet really in danger?" I asked him. "Or are you just for show?"

"Somebody left a death threat among his messages his first day here," Reju said. "Probably just a crank, but he got to thinking about what happened to John Lennon and called his manager. Who flew me down. I've been here a week, and nobody's made a move on Yonnet." Reju shrugged and added, in that dead-serious tone of his, "But that's all right—he's paying my top fee, either way."

Money was definitely one of the things Reju took most seriously.

"Who is the jumbo-size character at the bar?" I asked him.

"Name's Boyan Traikov."

"Bulgarian or Russian?"

"Bulgarian originally. But he came to France with his parents when he was just a kid."

"Where do you know him from?"

"Met him a couple of times when I was with a client at one of the gambling clubs owned by Didier Sabarly. He works for Sabarly."

Didier Sabarly was one of the current heavyweights of the Parisian underworld, with a range of interests that included loan-sharking and hard drugs as well as the illicit but well-protected gambling clubs. I asked Reju, "What does Traikov do for Sabarly? Muscle?"

"Started that way, but graduated. To straightening out problems that crop up in any of Sabarly's business. Don't be misled by his size. Traikov has a sharp brain in that thick head."

"Brain and brawn. Potent combination."

"Potent enough to move him up the ladder. High enough, from what I hear, so he never has to risk getting caught carrying a gun any more. Usually has somebody else along to take that risk for him."

"Any idea what he's doing down here?"

"None at all."

"He showed up this evening with Fulvio Callega's kid brother, Tony." I indicated Charles Jacquier's table outside. "The dashing fellow with the mustache."

"I didn't know Callega had a brother."

"What *do* you know about Fulvio Callega?"

Less than I did, it turned out. Nor did Reju have anything else of use to me. He looked at his watch. "Yonnet and his wife leave for the airport in a few minutes. Flying to London."

"Your job finished after you see them off?"

"Yes. But my room here in the hotel is paid until tomorrow noon. So I might as well use it: come back and enjoy a room-service dinner, get myself a good night of sleep. I haven't had much the last week. Serge Yonnet is a night owl."

I gave it a moment's thought. "If you're staying," I told him, "I've got a short job for you. Just to check on something."

I explained what I had in mind. Reju looked reluctant.

"I'm not asking for a personal favor," I said, "it's for a client. You'll get paid."

"How long do you want me on it?"

"A day, two days maximum. If nothing develops by then, my premise is wrong."

Reju nodded gravely. "All right."

"But not your *top* fee," I told him. "My client isn't *that* rich."

We were haggling over his fee when Serge Yonnet and his wife climbed out of their booth. Reju left me and preceded them through the lounge and into the hotel lobby.

A few minutes later the group at Jacquier's table broke up, shaking hands. Inside the bar the Bulgarian bruiser, Boyan Traikov, paid his bill and relieved the barstool of his considerable weight.

Jacquier and the two distributors left the terrace and parted on the pavement. Jacquier headed toward the Martinez. They went off in the opposite direction.

Traikov strolled out of the bar to join Tony Callega, who stood waiting for him. I strolled out after Traikov.

He and Tony Callega walked down off the terrace and turned away from the Croisette at Rue du Canada, the first side street leading into the interior of town. I followed them, keeping distance between us.

Traikov's towering hulk made them easy to follow.

▣ **14** ▣

TONY CALLEGA'S VILLA WAS NEAR THE EASTERN EDGE OF town, a few blocks in from the smaller of the two Cannes yacht harbors.

I'd lost him and Boyan Traikov minutes after leaving the Carlton. On the other side of the Rue d'Antibes, where traffic was easing off for the night, they'd walked into a garage and driven out in a sleek gray-blue Daimler Sovereign. With no taxi in sight, and my own car on the other side of the railroad station, all I could do about that was watch them go.

Tony Callega wasn't in the phone book, so I'd called the festival's information center. Sure enough, he'd listed himself there, complete with home address. I'd phoned Reju at the Carlton, but he wasn't back from the airport yet. Leaving a message for him, I had walked to my car and driven to Tony's address.

I parked around the block and walked back to his house. It wasn't big, as Cannes villas go. About ten rooms, I estimated. In that location it would sell for well over a million dollars. It was a contemporary two-level place in the middle of a garden enclosed by a high chain link fence topped with sharp spikes. The garden was overcrowded with giant cactus plants that loomed like misshapen monsters in the darkness under the palm trees.

Lights were on inside some of the villa's downstairs windows, but the sleek Daimler wasn't in the wide graveled driveway inside the steel-picket gate. Just a two-door Renault 5. But according to Chantal Jacquier, they would all be meeting there before going to dinner. If they hadn't already been and gone. I decided to give it half an hour. It didn't take that long.

I'd been waiting less than ten minutes, in the deep shadow of one of the cedars across the street, when Tony Callega arrived in the Daimler. He stopped in front of his gate and honked the horn.

Boyan Traikov was no longer with him.

Lights went on outside the villa's front door and atop the gateposts. A medium-sized man with a hawklike face came out of the house and unlocked the gate. Tony Callega drove in, got out of the Daimler, and spoke for a minute to him before going into the villa. Hawkface got in the Renault and drove out, leaving the gate open.

As the Renault went past my hiding place I could read its license number. I jotted it in my notebook for possible future reference. The car turned a corner and went its way, picking up speed.

A few minutes later Charles Jacquier and his daughter arrived in a Mercedes. Five minutes after they'd gone inside the villa another Mercedes pulled into the open gateway. The two distributors got out of the front seat, and a couple of women climbed from the back. As they went to the villa door I walked around the block to my Peugeot.

I cruised back past the villa. The three cars were still in the driveway. I parked at the end of the block, turned off my lights, and waited. Half an hour. Drinks before dinner, I guessed.

Then the Jacquier Mercedes came out, followed by the other one. The Daimler drove out last. Tony Callega stopped to relock his gate before driving after the first two cars.

My Peugeot was facing the wrong way. I did a U-turn with my headlights off, let the Daimler get a full block ahead, and then began to tail the three cars.

They turned away from Cannes and headed east along the coast road. There was just enough traffic there to make tailing easy. I switched on my parking lights and kept a few other cars between me and the Daimler. Now and then I checked my rearview mirror. But I couldn't tell if any of the cars back there were tailing *me*.

A few miles from Cannes we entered Juan-les-Pins, the

fashionable little resort town at the western base of Cap
d'Antibes. At night most of its activity is concentrated close
to the shore, where the posh restaurants and clubs huddle
between pine woods and beach. That was where the three
cars I was following went, turning into Avenue Guy de
Maupassant.

They pulled into the parking area of Les Mimosas, one
of the best and most expensive Basque restaurants on the
Riviera. I drove past and found a curbside space for my
Peugeot around the corner on Avenue Joffre.

Across from Les Mimosas there was a self-consciously
stylish brasserie with a shiny interior dominated by sculp-
tured aluminum and black mirrors. I used its phone to call
the Carlton and ask for Jean-Marie Reju. He'd been and
gone. I left another message and managed to get one of the
brasserie's window tables, with a view of Les Mimosas.
Which was some compensation for the tough gigot I had
for dinner while keeping watch.

When they came out Tony Callega gave Chantal Jacquier a brief good-night kiss and shook hands with the
others. Then he stood outside the restaurant, waving as
they drove out of the parking lot and back toward Cannes.
When they were gone he started walking briskly away from
the brightly lit section and into the dimmer interior of the
town.

I left the brasserie and tailed him. I looked back once to
check on whether *I* had a tail.

After five blocks the short, narrow streets became very
poorly lighted, with no other people at all in sight. Tony
Callega kept going past the dark post office building. It
wasn't until he entered a murky, deserted street by the
railroad line that he stopped and looked behind him.

I stepped into a recessed doorway in time to avoid his
spotting me. When I peeked out he'd stopped again; this
time beside a four-door Fiat parked by the mouth of a pedestrian tunnel that led under the train tracks.

Nobody was sitting in the car. But its front window had
been wound down and left that way, on the railroad side.
Tony Callega took an envelope from his pocket and tossed

it in through the open window. Then he hurried away, turning back toward the beach at the next corner.

I reached the Fiat and leaned down to look inside for the envelope. It wasn't in sight. What was there was a man of medium height with a hawklike face, who was lying on his back across the front seat. The one I'd seen leave Tony Callega's villa in a Renault.

He grinned up at me and said, "Put your hands on top of the car. And then don't move again, not at all."

His tensed, squeaky voice wasn't impressive. The pistol in his skinny hand did the impressing. It was fitted with an efficient silencer, its dark snout aimed at my chest, dead center.

I put my hands on the Fiat's roof. Someone came out of the tunnel behind me. I turned my head and saw the powerhouse bulk of Boyan Traikov.

It wasn't hard to tell the difference between him and a piece of good news.

⊠ 15 ⊠

IT HADN'T BEEN NECESSARY FOR THEM TO TAIL ME. ALL they'd had to do was wait and let Tony Callega lead me to them.

Well, I'd *wanted* to find out if Tony could be provoked into making a revealing move. That it had come so soon told me I was on the right track. Next problem: staying alive to follow up on what I'd learned.

Boyan Traikov said, "Maurice told you not to move." He had a deep, heavy voice, the slight Bulgarian accent giving it a peculiar emphasis. "He *will* shoot you if you don't obey."

The hawk-faced Maurice was sitting up now, keeping the pistol steady on me through the open car window. He had a look I'd seen on other men; the gun was as essential a part of him as the hand that held it.

I held still while Traikov began running his big hands over me, checking to make sure I wasn't wearing a weapon. "This doesn't have to get too serious," he said while he frisked me. "Unless I get the feeling you're stubborn. I figure you work for money. What you're working on now's earning it the hard way. Too hard, if you don't drop it."

He was down to checking my ankles. He straightened up. His tone stayed businesslike, calm and steady. "There's other jobs that'll pay you the same without getting you hurt. Or worse than hurt. Am I getting through to you?"

"Sure. You want me to stop bothering Tony. Do I have to stop looking for Odile Garnier, too?"

"I said *drop* it." Traikov's tone got a cutting edge. "*All* of it. But maybe you *are* stubborn."

I turned my head enough to look at him again. He was studying me thoughtfully. I said, "Not that stubborn. I just

didn't realize it was something that important—enough for
Didier Sabarly to worry about.''

Traikov's eyes narrowed. "I see you don't understand."

"Yes I do," I assured him fervently.

"I'll have to make sure you do. Sure you understand
how *bad* you don't want more of *this* job." Traikov closed
a hand around my upper arm and yanked me away from
the Fiat. As easily as if I weighed twenty pounds. He let
go of me and pointed a thick finger at the tunnel. "We'll
finish out talk in there."

I looked up and down the darkly shadowed street. I nodded and let my shoulders sag.

Maurice opened the car door and started to get out.

I swiveled on my left foot and rammed the heel of my
right against the car door. Maurice yelped in pain as he
slammed back inside the Fiat with one leg sticking out. I
swiveled back and drove my elbow up at Traikov's throat.

He jerked his head down and aside too quickly. My elbow missed his throat and chin, skidding across his mouth.
Blood spurted from his lower lip. I hit him in the gut, as
hard as I could. It was like punching an elephant. He just
grunted and got his own punch in. It struck me squarely in
the middle of my chest.

It wasn't as bad as getting hit by a truck, but near
enough. My heart spasmed, and I bounced off the Fiat's
hood. Traikov closed in. I tried to knee him in the valu-
ables, but I was still off balance. He took it on his hip and
his fist clubbed the side of my head.

I stumbled across the narrow sidewalk and fetched up
against the stone wall beside the tunnel. My brain was
clouding up on me, and there was a ringing inside the
cloud. I turned and braced my shoulders against the wall
to hold myself up. I didn't want to go down and get
stomped. Traikov's fists were bad enough. A full round
with him and I'd be punchy or crippled. Or both.

He came toward me, taking his time. His bleeding lip
was already puffing up. He wasn't invulnerable. But I knew
I'd never been up against anyone stronger. Plus he was fast
and knew all the moves.

Maurice was coming out of the car. I sidestepped from the wall, to keep Traikov's bulk between me and Maurice's pistol, and launched a kick at Traikov's knee. If I could tumble him against Maurice, and *if* I could snatch Maurice's gun . . .

But I'd become much too slow for any of it. Traikov stepped inside the kick and hit me again, this time just below the ribs. My knees bent to the pavement. I concentrated on getting back up and keeping my dinner down.

Maurice stepped around Traikov and aimed his pistol at my face. "Let me kill him," he whispered. There was passion in the whisper. He didn't have Traikov's business-like control. Stupidity and brutality rested comfortably together in Maurice's eyes.

"I didn't come down here to kill anybody," Traikov said reflectively. He stood there with his huge fists dangling, squinting at me and considering it. "But maybe it's necessary."

The cavalry finally arrived.

Jean-Marie Reju's flat voice had a quiet but unmistakable authority in it: "That's enough of that."

From my point of view, that was the understatement of the year.

Maurice spun around with his pistol and stopped himself just in time. If he'd turned another couple inches, he would have been dead.

Traikov turned just his head at first. He regarded Reju and the big Colt .45. Opening his hands, Traikov spread them away from his body, showing them empty. *Then* he turned the rest of his bulk to face Reju.

I leaned against the wall and worked at clearing the dark mist out of my head and vision. It was slow work.

Traikov nodded toward me and asked Reju, "Friend of yours?"

"Sort of," Reju admitted, and he told Maurice, "Put your gun down on the pavement and back away from it."

Maurice hesitated. Without his pistol he would be less than half a man.

"Do it!" Traikov snapped at him. "*This* guy'll put three bullets in your eye while you're still trying to get pointed in the right direction."

Maurice took a draggy breath and forced himself. He bent and laid the pistol on the pavement, straightened, and backed off a couple steps.

Reju asked me, without taking his attention off Traikov and Maurice, "Do you want to talk to them some more?"

I couldn't think of any trick questions that might net me more information. Not at that moment. My head was too swollen for that kind of effort. My chest and midsection ached horribly. I felt the thudding of my heart clear down to the soles of my feet. I took shallow breaths to keep from adding to the pain in my ribs, and I didn't risk shaking my head. I said, "No." My voice was all right.

"Walk away," Reju told Traikov and Maurice. "Through that tunnel. Don't come back here for at least an hour."

Traikov nodded. He looked at me and spoke in an even, reasonable tone. "I hope you did understand me. If you *don't* drop what you're working on, you'll need more than Reju to keep you alive."

He seized Maurice's arm, turned him away from his pistol, and dragged him into the tunnel. Reju watched them go off through its gloom, under the railroad tracks. Then he looked at me. "You don't look so good," he announced in a matter-of-fact tone.

"I'd look a lot better if you'd showed up sooner," I told him.

Reju looked mildly offended. "You *told* me to give you time to talk if they grabbed you. So I did. I've been behind you since you left that brasserie."

"I know, I spotted you," I said. "Maybe you didn't notice, but that gorilla stopped talking and started hitting a while back."

"He could have been roughing you up a little before talking some more," Reju pointed out. "He didn't hit you that much. It was the little one with the gun that got me worried."

I let it go. There was no point in hurting Reju's feelings

permanently. I moved away from the solid support of the wall and tested my legs. They held me up. "Let's go," I said.

Reju used a handkerchief to pick up Maurice's pistol, stepped off the curb, and dropped it down a storm drain. Then he walked me back in the direction of the beach, holding his .45 down against his thigh. I took it slow. With every step a throb expanded from my chest and sounded against the inside of my skull. Like someone giving a light kick to a bass drum. Reju matched his pace to mine with a phlegmatic expression that didn't signify any relaxation of vigilance. He had his faults, but impatience was not one of them.

I stopped when we reached the first bar. "I need a drink."

He slid the big Colt into its holster under his raincoat and followed me inside. I ordered brandy. Reju asked for a drink of water—from the tap. Bottled water costs money, but bars are required by law to supply a free drink of ordinary water to anyone who needs it.

The brandy helped. Reju drank his free water and said, "My room has twin beds. You can use the other one, if you need to."

"That's good of you," I told him.

He nodded, agreeing it was good of him. I considered his offer. The night was still young, but I was in no condition to accomplish anything more with it. Besides, the people I wanted to see next were off working at night. Reju's room was temptingly close, but I thought I could manage the drive home—and the way I felt, home was where I wanted to be.

"Just convoy me to my car," I said. I paid for my brandy and left a tip for both of us.

When we got to the Peugeot he watched with a disapproving frown as I took my emergency pistol from its hidden compartment inside the back seat. It was a Heckler & Koch P7. It cost me some extra pain to holster it under my left arm before settling behind the steering wheel.

Reju bent down and told me, "You're taking a terrible

risk if the police catch you carrying that without a permit, Pierre-Ange.''

"Not as terrible as what I'd risk *not* carrying it—after what just happened."

He shrugged somberly. "You could lose your right to work in France, you know."

"I can't afford *you* all the time, Jean-Marie."

That reminded him: "Shall I mail you my bill for today?"

I nodded wearily. "But not for the whole day. I didn't use you for more than a couple hours."

"You know I don't have hourly rates." He considered it. "All right, since it's you, I'll only charge for half a day."

We agreed on that, and he stepped back and watched me drive off.

I took the autoroute because that was fastest. But I stuck to the right-hand lane all the way, in case I started to black out and had to pull over. I didn't.

An hour after leaving Reju I was tucked into the comforting familiarity of my house, feeding myself a codeine. I filled the bathtub with water at body-temperature, poured in *huile d'arnica* for the bruises, and soaked for half an hour. By then the codeine was making the aches and pains seem somewhat remote. I drenched some big gauze pads with more of the *huile d'arnica* and fastened them on the worst of the bruises.

Then I crawled into bed and floated off into a blissful, stoned sleep.

When I got up next morning my neck was stiff, but the bruises had become localized and less painful. I took two aspirins with my breakfast, followed by a lukewarm shower. A third cup of coffee and I was functional enough to make a few phone calls.

The first was to Egon Mulhausser. He hadn't heard anything from or about his daughter.

My call to Fritz didn't get me much more. None of the other students he'd talked to so far at the College de France knew where Odile was—nor much of anything else about her. They said she'd been pretty much of a loner. Fritz hadn't yet been able to pinpoint the troglodyte group that had sent her the postcard. A burglar he knew had gotten inside her apartment the previous night, but he hadn't found an address book or anything else that might give us a lead to investigate.

"About Tony Callega," Fritz told me. "I haven't turned up any indication of his having criminal connections here in Paris. His friends seem to be confined to the sort of well-to-do people who inhabit the sixteenth *arrondissement*, where his apartment is located. The BCBGs."

The *bon chic, bon genre* crowd—BCBG for short—is the fashionable Parisian set, people from good families. Always stylishly dressed and always seen at the latest in places. Never at places that *used* to be in. Cynics say such social blunders are prevented by special detection instruments implanted at birth, where souls used to be. The BCBGs are clannish and resent social climbers. Which led me to speculate on how a Tony Callega had managed to get accepted by them. Not money, as in the case of Charles Jacquier. BCBGs are never short of funds.

Information on the other names I'd given Fritz was beginning to trickle in from his myriad telephone contacts. Including, from his connections in Italy, some little-known background on Fulvio Callega—personal as well as professional. Some of which inclined Fritz to instigate further in-depth inquiries in such unexpected places as Florida and Hong Kong.

But nothing that helped us locate Odile Garnier.

I gave Fritz two more names to research—Didier Sabarly and Boyan Traikov—and explained why.

My final call was to Arlette in London, to ask how the conference with her father's doctors had turned out. There was an undercurrent of anxiety in her voice, though she had it under control. Her father was in considerable pain, she told me, and a decision had been made to risk operating on him in a couple of days.

I had a certain amount of grudging attachment to Marcel

Alfani myself. I didn't let that delude me into feeling the old gangster's death, whenever it came, would be any loss to humanity. His contributions to the world could be counted on two fingers: He had helped my mother escape from the Gestapo during the war, and he was Arlette's father. Otherwise his life had inflicted as much unpleasantness as that of a Fulvio Callega or Didier Sabarly. But I gave Arlette all the sympathy I could manage via a long-distance phone call.

Then I strapped on the Heckler & Koch under my Levi's jacket, got in my car, and went back to work.

⊠ 16 ⊠

THE CORK OAK WHERE ANDRÉ MARCHINE MET ME WAS IN the densely wooded volcanic hills of the Esterel Massif, nine miles west of Cannes.

The tree was ancient and had been dead for the last half century. The iron spike protruding from its trunk was bent and encrusted with rust. According to local legend, the head of the notorious bandit, Gaspard de Besse, had been nailed to that tree with that spike after he'd been captured and beheaded two hundred years ago.

Having that on his land didn't seem to bother André Marchine. He wasn't superstitious, which is as unusual for a professional criminal as it is for a professional actor.

The tree was at the bottom of his property, beside a dirt road that wound through the sloped forests and farms. The road was as red as the boulders and rock formations looming out of the green of the pines and fruit trees. The Esterel Massif is thick with iron oxide.

André's battered old Renault 4 van was parked by the cork oak. I pulled up behind it as he emerged from the abandoned farmhouse he'd restored with his own hands. He came down the crooked red path, a man of sixty now, tall and bald, with a deeply seamed face.

I got out of my car and he hugged me. "It's been a long time, Pierre-Ange."

"Almost a year," I said. "You're looking better than you did then."

That was true. His cheeks had color, and his eyes were clear. He was still thin, but there was some meat on his bones now.

"I haven't touched any hard drugs in all that time," he

said with a shy, proud smile. "Just some hash or marijuana, now and then. And not too much of that, either."

His pride was justified. The last time I'd seen him he had been fighting his way out of a long-time addiction to heroin. And doing it the most painful way possible: cold turkey, with no medical help at all. I'd stayed with him through a week of that. One of the worst weeks of my life—but much worse for him.

That had been several months after I'd helped prove him innocent of taking part in the armed holdup of a bank. I'd been certain he would never use a gun. He wasn't a violent type of criminal; it just wasn't in him. André Marchine was into milder forms of thievery: forging other people's names on stolen checks and credit card vouchers.

Before that he'd been a teacher at the Cap d'Ail grade school. Back when I'd first known him. It was his getting hooked on heroin that had turned him into a criminal. That was the only way he could earn enough to support his habit. And it had been Petar, the boy he'd adopted as his son, who'd finally given him the incentive—and the incredible willpower—to break the addiction. He'd gotten frightened the boy would pick up the habit from him.

We climbed the path together. The only sound was the buzzing of bees gorging themselves in the wild honeysuckle vines.

It was late morning of my second day since I'd been waylaid by Traikov and Maurice. The day before had been a total loss. I'd spent that morning showing Odile Garnier's picture around Villefranche. There were people who recognized her face, but none of them could give me anyone who knew her better than that. Then I'd spent that afternoon, evening, and much of the night talking to small-fry members of the underworld *milieu* I knew in Nice and Cannes, probing for the connection between Tony Callega, Bruno Ravic, and Odile Garnier. I'd come up empty.

André Marchine was my latest try, and I was hoping he would prove more forthcoming.

His house had been constructed for defense, back in the last century. The Esterel had been a favorite hiding place

for convicts who escaped from the Toulon hulks. Many of
them had joined together in bands that, like the famed de
Besse, had continued to make the entire massif an area
sensible travelers avoided. Its dangerous reputation hadn't
changed until after the turn of the century.

The thick stone wall of the ground floor had no windows
or door. Only several small loopholes. The door of the
house was on the floor above. It could only be reached by
a narrow stone stairway built into the front wall. André led
me up the steps and inside.

He stopped halfway along the inner corridor to look inside a small bedroom. Petar was in the bed, asleep. The
boy was twelve now. He'd been ten when Andre had pur-
chased him.

According to Interpol's figures, thousands of children
have been bought from impoverished families in Yugoslavia and smuggled into the West by syndicates that train
the kids as pickpockets before offering them for sale to
professionals like André Marchine. One of the strongest
syndicates is headquartered in Amsterdam. That was where
André had gotten Petar.

Before then, André's stolen checks and credit cards had
been supplied by thieves out of what they found in snatched
purses and looted houses. They charged high prices, considering that he had to use the checks and cards very
quickly, before the fact that they had been stolen showed
up in all the computers. André had finally decided it would
be more economical to get his own thief.

The Amsterdam syndicate that had sold him Petar had
also supplied Dutch government forms stating that André
was the boy's official adoptive father. The adoption papers
were phony of course. But André and Petar had come to
care for each other as though they *were* father and son.
Another anxiety that had begun tormenting André the last
I'd seen him was the risk of the police catching the boy
and putting him in a home for delinquent kids.

André shut the bedroom door quietly and led me on toward the rear of the house. "Petar's had a fever the last

couple of days," he told me. "I've had to keep him home from school."

"School?"

André nodded. "In Cannes. I take him in the morning and bring him back in the afternoon." He looked just a bit embarrassed. "I don't let him work anymore. I couldn't take the anxiety. Worrying about the cops separating us. Petar needs me . . . and I need him."

"That mean you're back to sharing half your profits with outside thieves?"

"Yes, but that's not as bad as the worry. And I don't *need* as much money anymore, now that I don't have to pay for my habit."

"If you don't need that much money now, you ought to go back to teaching."

"*That* doesn't pay enough to take care of Petar's future education. No, I'm saving up to buy a little souvenir shop in Nice."

"I hope you make that switch before the cops catch *you*," I said. "Or you won't be able to do *anything* for Petar."

"*Please*," André begged, "don't make me more neurotic about that than I already am."

"I've got a little money in savings right now," I told him. "If you don't need much more to get the place in Nice, I could give you a short-term loan."

"No," he said, with that perverse but genuine dignity of his. "Though I do thank you for the offer. I want to do it on my own. As I've done everything else in my life— good and bad."

We went down the back steps to a huge old-fashioned kitchen that was also dining and living room. André had installed full-sized windows in the back wall there. They looked across a wide ravine of red stone spires and dark Maritime pines.

"Coffee?"

I nodded, and André went to the stove to prepare it. The stove was one of the better brands. So were the other appliances. André seldom risked going to a bank with his checks and credit cards. He preferred to buy things with them. Most of what he acquired that way was resold to a fence in Cannes. But some things he kept.

When we were seated at the table with our cups of *café crème* I pushed one of my photos of Odile Garnier across to him. "Ever seen her around?"

André studied her face. "No." I told him her name, but that didn't mean anything to him either. I tried the closeup of the boy who'd been in the other snapshot with her. Another blank.

"The girl was with Bruno Ravic for a while," I told him. "What do you know about *him*?"

He cocked an eyebrow at me: "I know what happened to him."

"Including who killed him?"

"No, that I don't know."

"I'm interested in before he got killed. I figured you might know some background stuff on him."

"You mean because he was from Yugoslavia, and so is Petar?" André shook his head. "If Ravic was ever involved with smuggling the kids out of there, it's news to me."

"I mean because he was involved in supplying dope—and you were a user."

"We never had any contact," André told me. "But I did *hear* things about him."

"Like what?"

"Ravic wasn't a dealer. Not a pusher, either. The word was he was a transporter. Used to carry supplies from here up to Paris. That's nothing I can swear to, understand. Merely something I heard."

It sounded right. It would fit with pieces I'd been putting together. "Did what you heard include the name of the Paris buyer?"

André shook his head. "No idea."

"What about Didier Sabarly?"

"As the buyer in Paris? It's *possible*."

"What do you think of Fulvio Callega as the supplier Ravic carried the drugs for?"

"That's possible, too. But I just don't *know*."

I tried the name of Boyan Traikov on André, but it didn't mean anything to him.

We were interrupted by Petar, who came down the back steps in his pajamas and slippers. He gave me a sleepy stare, saying politely, "*Bonjour, Monsieur*." Then he climbed onto André's lap and reached for his coffee.

André pushed the cup away from him. "Caffeine isn't good for you right now." He kissed Petar on the forehead, letting his lips stay there for a moment. "But I think your temperature is down."

"I'm thirsty."

"I'll get you some orange juice." André sat the boy on his chair and went to fill a glass with juice. He brought it back and said, "Drink it in your bed, and I'll be up soon to take your temperature. Monsieur Sawyer and I are having a private discussion."

Petar nodded and went back up the steps with his orange juice. No sign of reluctance. He'd spent enough of his life in a world where "private discussions" were respected.

When he was gone I asked André, "Do you know Tony Callega?"

"Not personally. I know a bit *about* him. The same as with Ravic: only things I've heard from other people."

"He and Ravic were involved in something together," I told him. "It could have been drugs. Heard anything along that line?"

"You mean is Tony Callega involved with dope on a commercial basis? I don't think so. The word around is that his brother doesn't want him mixed up in anything too illegal."

That, too, fitted everything I'd learned so far.

"Of course," André added, "he does have *access* to drugs. Coke, heroin, pills—anything some of the jet set might run short of when they're down here. According to my information, Tony can always supply whatever they need—or tell them where to get it. But not for money. To ingratiate himself with them, I guess. The same reason he supplies girls."

That reminded me of my speculation about how Tony Callega had gotten in with the Parisian BCBGs. "Girls—do you mean call girls?"

"No, just plain *girls*." André smiled a little. "Actually, girls who aren't plain. But not whores. Just those beautiful young things who pour down from all over the world to the Riviera beaches every year to get a feeling of glamour with their suntans. According to my source, that's where Tony picks some of them up. Along the beaches. And then maybe gets them high on something and feeds them to his jet set friends."

"Who's your source?"

André hesitated and then remembered he could trust me. "My cousin. Josette. She has a place Tony Callega drops into once in a while, outside St. Tropez. A disco bar near the beach. The Casbah. Do you know it?"

I didn't. He told me how to find it.

⊠ 17 ⊠

BRIGITTE BARDOT DID FOR ST. TROPEZ WHAT COLUMBUS did for America. But the mass immigration that followed her discovery is strictly seasonal. St. Tropez is on the side of a cape facing north. It's one of the few resorts along the Riviera that gets unpleasantly cold all through wintertime. That's when St. Tropez shrinks back into a sleepy little fishing village, and the beaches outside it become as deserted as the Sahara.

But by May the mass invasion of vacationers has swelled the village to bursting with eccentrically clad visitors, and the beaches are packed to capacity with unclad flesh. On the St. Tropez beaches—Les Salins, Tahiti, La Bouillabaisse and Pampelonne—topless long ago gave way to over-all.

The bodies carpeting the sand of the public *plages* belong to young people short of cash. The rich get their tans beside hotel pools or on the decks of the yachts anchored close offshore. Where they can roll over without mixing their sweat with that of the strangers on either side of them.

The two classes do meet, and sometimes mingle, in places like the Casbah, after the sun goes down. The rich search for low-down adventure, and the poor for someone who might stake them to a square meal, or even a longer stay.

The Casbah was about three hundred yards from Tahiti Plage. There was one large room with a bar, tables, and a dance space. It was open on one side to a thatch-shaded courtyard with more tables and dance space, enclosed on three sides by a picket fence through which you could see the beach, the sea, and the yachts. The Casbah's speakers were blaring hard rock, inside and out. But it was too early for most people to abandon the sun. The courtyard was empty, and the room inside almost so.

There were only two young couples dancing to the blare. The boys wore brief monokinis. One of the girls had on a full-length skirt of separate blue-plastic ropes. The other wore a cowboy hat and boots, and nothing between them— not that unusual a sight around St. Tropez. All four of them were Scandinavian blonds, and badly sunburned, which probably accounted for their seeking shade.

The only other customer was a pale middle-aged man in flowered sport shirt, bermuda shorts, and plastic sandals. He was at the bar, working on a dry martini and watching the two girls with shy hunger. Or it may have been the boys he was watching. It's often hard to tell. Sometimes even those who hunger aren't sure.

I was at the far end of the bar with André Marchine's cousin, Josette. Her last name was Beltoise, but André's phone call had put us on a relaxed first-name basis. Josette was a strongly built, pretty woman in her forties, with the kind of dark skin that is stocked with enough natural oils to withstand the ravages of sun and wind. With a few hours to go before her evening customers began filling the Casbah, she was able to give me her full attention.

She looked at the closeup picture of Odile Garnier for a while before giving me an answer. "If you hadn't just mentioned Tony Callega, I probably wouldn't remember. I get so many girls like this one in here, all summer and every summer. But yes—I've seen her. With him."

"Often?"

"No. Say four or six times—spread over a couple of years."

Egon Mulhausser's rough try at making Tony Callega keep away from his daughter hadn't worked too well. Or had worked in reverse. It could be Tony Callega's way of thumbing his nose at Mulhausser. Odile's, too. Protecting daughters from predators—and from themselves—gets harder all the time.

"Did they just happen to run into each other here?" I asked Josette. "Or would they come in together?"

"Together. Except the last time. That was about a month ago. Tony was with a guy I saw him with a few times before. They'd meet here, have a drink, look over the girls, and then go off somewhere together." Josette tapped the snapshot of Odile. "This time *she* came in while they were here. She sat at their table and started arguing with Tony."

"About what?"

"I couldn't hear. It *looked* like she wanted something from him—pretty badly. And Tony was telling her no. But finally the other guy started talking to her—and in the end she went out with *him*. She didn't look too happy about it. The guy did. And Tony—he watched them go with a funny kind of smile. Like he'd done something he got a nasty kick out of."

"You don't know who this other guy is."

"No. A good-looking tough type. Big as you."

I described Bruno Ravic.

"Yes—that could be him."

"What about the *first* time you saw Tony Callega with her?" I asked. "Did they come in together then—or was it a pickup that time?"

Josette thought about it and gave up. "I don't remember. He *could* have come in that time and just seen her and picked her up. That would fit the way he operates. Cruises along the coast in his boat. Anchors off the beach. Comes in with a dinghy and prowls around looking for fresh meat. The fresher ones are what he's after. Some of them he finds on the beach I wouldn't let in here. I draw the line at kids under fifteen."

"He likes them *that* young?"

"I don't know if *he* does. But some of his friends do. He's got friends with all kinds of tastes. Only thing they've got in common, I guess, is their money. And being, quote, respectable, unquote. Tony Callega picks up a girl, uses her for a short while, and then passes her to one of the friends. Sometimes he doesn't even use them himself before passing them on. Maybe that's his kink.''

"Or his way of cementing friendships."

"That, too, sure. One girl he picked up in here told me about it later. Tony took her out to his boat along with an English girl he found on the beach. A kid of thirteen or fourteen. He gave them some coke to snort. Took them to Cannes. Both girls wound up in a little orgy, high on more coke, with some men who had very special sexual preferences.

"Another girl I knew, after Tony Callega picked her up she started showing up here the rest of the summer with a man old enough to be my grandfather. He'd sit and watch her dance with the boys. When that got him turned on enough, he'd take her back out to his yacht."

"It doesn't sound like the girls objected to any of this too much."

Josette's laugh was wry. "Of course not. So many of those kids—boys and girls alike—they get down here having spent the last of their money for their fare. What're they hoping for, after all? Somebody to finance the rest of their vacation. So who's to complain?"

"What kind of boat has Tony Callega got?" I asked her.

"Big cabin cruiser. But not too big for one man to handle. Though he sometimes has another guy helping with it. Comes in with him in the dinghy. Scrawny guy with a bony face and a big beak."

That sounded very much like Maurice. "Know the name of his boat?"

She laughed again. "How could I forget it? *Prince Antoine*—that's what he named it. One thing you've got to hand Tony Callega, he doesn't suffer from an overabundance of modesty."

Josette didn't know of anyone, other than Tony, who was acquainted with Odile Garnier. But she'd given me considerable food for thought. I thanked her, went out to my car, and drove back to Cannes.

Three small airplanes of 1920s vintage were flying low over the Croisette, trailing banners promoting an Italian producer's next historical sex-and-muscles epic. There was a ten-piece band outside the Palais des Festivals playing numbers from a new Hollywood musical. I walked past the Palais and along the Quai St. Pierre, on one side of the main Cannes yacht harbor. The *Prince Antoine* was moored near the end of it.

It would have been interesting to find Maurice there. He'd probably gotten himself another gun by then—but I had one of my own this time. Nobody was aboard, however. I stood there for a while, looking at Tony's cabin cruiser, speculating on what it could be used for, besides seduction and other forms of amusement.

It wasn't as big as some of the floating mansions docked near it—but big enough to suggest certain possibilities.

The authorities didn't pay much attention to the movements of yachts they were familiar with. With thousands of them along the Côte d'Azur, it would be impossible to conduct a search every time one of them came back from a half day's pleasure cruise.

Tony Callega would run very little risk if he sailed his boat out over the horizon and met a vessel from Italy. And took a shipment of drugs from his big brother. Which he brought back and turned over to someone like Bruno Ravic. Who carried it up to Paris, where it was delivered to Didier Sabarly's people.

Pure speculation.

But intriguing.

And quite possible.

I walked back along the quay, past the Palais and the ten-piece band, and went into the nearest bar at that end of the Croisette. I used its rear phone booth to call Tony Callega's villa. No response. Tony wasn't there, and neither was Maurice.

I called Charles Jacquier at the Martinez. He wasn't there. He'd left word he would return in a couple of hours. Next I tried Chantal Jacquier. She wasn't in her suite, but when she was paged she picked up the call in the hotel's cocktail lounge.

Giving my French a strong American accent, I identified myself as a Hollywood producer and explained that I was trying to get in touch with either her father or his associate, Antoine Callega, about an urgent negotiation. Her father, Chantal told me, was closeted somewhere with a screen star he hoped to use in his new picture. Tony Callega had gone out of town on business the previous morning. She didn't know what the business was, but she *thought* it was in Paris.

I began calling hotels and asking for Boyan Traikov, trying the best hotels first. I hit it on the fourth try: Traikov had stayed at the Majestic, for one night. He'd checked out the morning before. Leaving no word about where he was going.

That gave me something specific to worry about. Tony Callega had been seeing Odile Garnier over the last two years. He had to know more about her than I did. His sudden departure from Cannes, along with Boyan Traikov, could mean they had a lead on Odile's whereabouts.

I gave the bar's cashier a fifty-franc note for ten five-franc coins. Going back to the phone booth, I plugged in several of them, dialed the code for Paris, and then dialed the number of Tony Callega's apartment—one of the items Fritz Donhoff had dredged up for me.

Tony Callega picked up on the second ring, sounding uptight. I altered my voice just enough and charged it with angry urgency. "Sabarly told me to call and see if you're making *any* progress in finding that girl."

"I *told* him we'd—" Tony Callega stopped himself abruptly. There was a short silence, and then another voice came on.

"Who is this?"

An unmistakable voice: Boyan Traikov.

I hung up on him. My hunch had been correct. They'd gone to Paris. That had to mean they'd gotten some kind of lead on Odile Garnier there. And they had been up there following it for almost two days.

I dropped in more coins, phoned Fritz Donhoff, and told him to clamp a watch on Tony Callega's apartment. "If they come out before I get there, I want them tailed. Two men, two cars—in case they split up."

I drove to the Côte d'Azur airport and got on the next flight to Paris.

⊠ **18** ⊠

Fritz Donhoff was waiting for me inside the terminal at Orly Airport. A big, heavy man with meticulously brushed silver hair and a large, baggy-eyed face. Dressed as always with a dignified old-world elegance. He had bad news.

"Tony Callega and Boyan Traikov. They left the apartment before I could stake it out. I phoned—no answer."

"Merde."

Fritz remained unruffled. "I have a man watching the apartment. If either of them returns, he'll let us know immediately."

"They might not come back. If it was my call that made them leave that suddenly, they shifted someplace else. Have you been able to get Traikov's address?"

"He's cagey about that. Seems he has more than one residence in Paris. Nobody's at the one I know about. But," Fritz added as we left the terminal building, "a couple new items came my way shortly after your call from Cannes."

The evening sky outside was obscured by a low canopy of clouds. I was dressed too lightly for the chill breeze that blew as we walked toward the parking area.

"First of all," Fritz said, "there is a rumor going around certain Paris circles. Concerning Didier Sabarly. His organization was expecting a shipment of uncut heroin that didn't arrive. Hijacked somewhere along the line. Three million dollars' worth."

I took a slow breath. "Three million—uncut, that would fit in a knapsack."

"It *would* explain why Bruno Ravic tried so violently to escape the police," he acknowledged judiciously. "A violence not justified by the small amount of heroin found afterward in his apartment. Unless he had much more there—and thought it was *still* there. But the girl would have to be insane to steal something like that.''

"Or desperate.''

Fritz turned his handsome, aging face to give me a questioning look. "You have some new evidence indicating Odile Garnier is an addict?''

"Not evidence,'' I admitted, "but it's a strong possibility.'' I told Fritz about Tony Callega's habit of getting girls zonked on dope before pushing them to his friends. And about him apparently passing Odile on to Bruno Ravic.

"She was a special case for Tony,'' I said. "A couple years ago he made a pass at her, and her father warned him off the rough way. And he's been seeing her since. It would fit what I know of his character to deliberately get her hooked on heroin, as a vicious way of getting even.''

"That is not a strong possibility,'' Fritz admonished me, like a wise old teacher dealing with a bright but over-hasty student. It was one of the roles he fell into now and then. I usually humored him, because he *had* stored up a lot of wisdom over his seven decades. "It is merely an *assumption*.''

"It *assumes* Bruno worked for Fulvio Callega,'' I agreed. "And that Fulvio Callega is the supplier of that shipment Didier Sabarly was expecting. We may not have hard proof of that, but it *does* fit the circumstances.''

"You are also assuming that Odile Garnier knew Bruno had just gotten that new shipment for delivery to Sabarly. And that she *is* an addict.''

"She can't *sell* that much heroin,'' I pointed out. "The kind of people who buy that quantity would inform Sabarly. She can't be dumb enough to think otherwise. So if she didn't take it to sell, she took it to use.''

"Which is only a little less stupid.''

"You mix addiction with desperation, and it doesn't add up to playing it safe,'' I said. "She saw her chance to get a lifetime supply—and grabbed it.''

"I hope you're wrong." Fritz spoke with a heavy, deliberate calm. I'd never seen him anything but calm and deliberate, in any situation. "Because if you're right, her lifetime is likely to become extremely short."

"If I'm right, that might not bother her much." I was remembering what André Marchine had once told me. For an addict, the concept of a lifetime means the hours between your last fix and your next one. Any life beyond that becomes unreal, and difficult to regard as important.

Fritz unlocked his car and got in behind the wheel. As I slid in beside him he said, "We'll stop at your apartment so you can get into something warmer."

"I appreciate the thought."

He smiled and patted my knee with a fatherly fondness. "I have to take care of you, my boy."

Since my real father had died before I was born, Fritz *was* as close to one as I would ever know. "You said you had a *couple* of new items," I reminded him as he drove out of Orly and onto the highway to Paris. "Sabarly's missing shipment is one."

"The other is a young woman named Karine Vidal. She belongs to a club of weekend troglodytes. The Catacomb Crawlers, they call themselves."

I didn't let my spirits lift too much. Fritz would have mentioned it immediately, if it was a hot lead. I was right.

"She doesn't know our Odile Garnier," Fritz told me. "But she does recognize the closeup of the boy who was in the other picture with Odile. Karine has seen him several times when her group was playing its underground games. She doesn't know his name or anything else about him— nor does any other member or her club. But she *is* certain the boy in the photograph is the one they ran into."

It wasn't much. But it *was* the first thing we'd gotten that just might put us on Odile's recent trail. "If *he's* an undercity explorer," I said, "somebody else down there is bound to know more about him."

Fritz nodded. "And this is Friday, the night most of

them play their underground games.'' He spared me a bland smile. ''That is another reason I'm glad you're here—in addition to my usual pleasure in seeing you at any time. *I* wouldn't relish being the one who has to spend the night crawling through the intestines of Paris.''

Karine Vidal and I took the Métro to Babylon.

She'd agreed with my interpretation of the postcard Odile Garnier had received, and added a thought of her own:

''I never heard of anything in that exact area. So somebody must have discovered a new underground complex. And if it's new, they may still be exploring it, even if the card was sent last month.''

I'd offered to pay for her help, but she'd said no to that. She had a good job in the insurance business. That was her work, this was her pleasure. She was with me because the idea of helping an American private eye turned her on. Fritz had stressed the American part of that, because it made me exotic to her. Karine Vidal obviously dug the exotic.

She was in her mid-twenties, tall and large-boned, with a plump, freckled face and a small, cautious smile. There was nothing else cautious about her appearance that Friday night. She hadn't been able to meet me until after nine because she'd had to devote a few hours to converting herself from a conservative young businesswoman into an outrageous punk. Weekends were her time to howl.

Like many punks, Karine Vidal was too shy to *act* outrageous. Her escapes into the alternate life-style were concentrated on looking the part.

She wore tight pink stretch pants, black motorcycle boots glistening with sequins, and a short blouson of fun fur dyed purple with gold streaks. The belt and bracelets were thick leather studded with nail heads. Her fair hair stuck out from her skull in waxed points. Her eyebrows were tinted yellow, her lipstick was fire-engine red, her nails were varnished black. Her earrings were small chain links from which dangled miniature handcuffs. The shoulder bag she carried was glossy blue plastic.

The other passengers on the Métro train were too busy looking at her to pay any attention to me. I'd put on a crew neck pullover and heavy-duty denim slacks, with a lightly padded field jacket. I was wearing sensible shoes with ribbed rubber soles and a corduroy cap, in case the heavy night clouds meant business. Very square, next to Karine Vidal.

She didn't mind that. I was her secret. Nobody else knew I was Sam Spade.

My field jacket was one size to large for me. Large enough to prevent any telltale bulge giving away the holstered gun under my left arm. It wasn't my Riviera H&K. Wearing a concealed gun without a permit to carry was always a risk—but one sometimes justified by circumstances. Nothing would have justified the additional risk of trying to carry one through airport controls. The gun in my shoulder holster Friday night was the one I kept hidden in my Paris apartment. A compact model Beretta 92SB, with fourteen 9mm cartridges snugly stacked in its magazine.

I didn't expect to run into characters like Traikov and Maurice searching underneath Paris. But it was possible. And an eventual encounter with the opposition was more than possible. I was looking for Odile's friends—and Tony Callega might already know who some of them were.

The Babylon Métro station has two exits. When we came up from the train we tried the nearest one first.

It surfaced at the intersection of Boulevard Raspail and Rue de Sèvres. Karine stopped and looked around. The Banque de France was on the other side of the intersection, across from the Lutetia, the Left Bank's best hotel. The corner nearest to us held the Babylon Bar. But those didn't interest Karine. She was studying the sidewalks.

"Nothing here," she announced. "When somebody finds a new way down they usually leave some kind of sign for others to follow. Let's try the other exit."

We went back down the steps, through the station, and up the stairway at the other end. That brought us into the open on the short, narrow Rue Velpeau, across from one side of the Bon Marché, a department store that spreads over three blocks. Karine pointed at the sidewalk. "There it is." It was a small emblem done with fluorescent orange paint: a circle with an arrow through it.

She led the way, going where the arrow pointed. After thirty steps we found another little circle-and-arrow. It was beside a stairwell to an underground public parking garage. "This is the way down," she said, "but there must be another way out." She nodded at a sign announcing that the garage was locked between 11:30 at night and 6:30 in the morning. "It's after midnight you get the most activity under the city. But nobody wants to get trapped down there until morning."

We descended the stairwell. It ended at the fifth level down. The parking spaces, silent and ill-lit, held few cars at that hour. Karine got the flashlight out of her shoulder bag, and we reconnoitered the fifth level. We didn't have far to look. Half of the concrete floor had been ripped up. A ladder led down to where a sixth parking level was being excavated.

We used the ladder, and Karine swung her flashlight beam around. It steadied on a side wall of rough stone where the excavation had broken into one end of a low tunnel.

Parisians often come upon finds like that while digging their cellars deeper. Below the surface, the city is honey-combed with miles of forgotten passages and caverns. The remains of burial catacombs. Ancient quarries. Crypts of long-demolished churches. Old secret tunnels and sealed-up storage places. Abandoned aqueduct sections. Access routes dug by the workers who built the Métro and drainage systems. Maintenance shafts for the city's gas, electric, and telephone lines. Plus myriad other tunnels and chambers whose purpose no one any longer remembers.

"That must be it," Karine said as she crouched and

shone her flashlight into the low tunnel. Her small smile was a touch self-conscious as she added, "What we call a *Trou Noir*." A Black Hole—the way into an alternate universe.

I crawled in after her.

▨ **19** ▨

IT WASN'T A LONG CRAWL. THE TUNNEL RAN STRAIGHT
for about fifteen feet, and then we were out the other end.

We stood up in what appeared to have been the bottom
section of an underground military bunker. Perhaps an
emergency command shelter built between the World Wars.
Floor, walls, and ceilings of reinforced concrete. All that
remained were several partitions and some small holes in
the floor where latrines had been.

There were also some communications cables, dangling
on one wall next to rusting metal rungs that had led up to
a shaft above. The shaft was now sealed off with a thick
sheet of steel. In the opposite wall was a doorway. It, too,
had been closed up, with an iron door. But someone had
broken its lock, and the door now hung open.

We went through it into a dark passage that had been
cut long ago through the chalky stone on which the city
was built. The passage was high enough for us to walk
upright, wide enough for us to advance side by side. I had
expected a certain amount of sewage smell, but there was
none. The air was damp but clean, with just a faint tang
from the calcium contents of the stone around us. We
walked for what I judged to be the equivalent of a city
block, and then I was stopped by what sounded like an
approaching hurricane.

''Métro train,'' Karine Vidal told me.

It went past, the noise reverberating through the thick-
ness of the intervening stone. Inside the passage it was
impossible to tell if the train was to our right or left or
above. After it was gone the silence once more became as
solid as the darkness pierced by Karine's flashlight beam.

We reached a fork in the passage. Taking the right fork

first, we came after a few minutes to a dead end. It had
been blocked there with stones and cement. Somebody had
been at work on the blockage with a chisel but hadn't broken through. We retraced our steps and tried the other passage.

Wandering around the labyrinth under Paris—except with
a guided tour of a small section of the catacombs or sew-
ers—is forbidden by law. It's one of those laws the French
ignore—including the police, who have only two men assigned to check the thousands of subterranean corridors.
The cops had come to regard people like Karine Vidal as
useful sources of information about what goes on down
there. I knew of two arms caches and a dead body that
would never have been found otherwise.

Karine and I had been following the second passageway
for perhaps two blocks when I heard a peculiar whispering
sound. It echoed softly from somewhere ahead. I couldn't
identify it.

The passage made a sharp turn and then opened into a
vault enclosing a large pool. In the beam of the flashlight
its surface reflected like a rippled black mirror. Around the
water's edge a natural flooring of rough rock supported
heavy, crumbling arches built of small blocks of trimmed
stone. These in turn supported a low domed roof. It was
part of a subterranean reservior of the Middle Ages.

The sound I'd heard was the water. It was in slow, swirl-
ing motion pushed by some underwater source on one side
and flowing under the rock flooring on the other side.

We went around the water to an arched stone doorway.
On either side of it someone had recently stenciled life-
sized nude silhouettes in white. Male on one side, female
on the other, posed in the movements of a dance.

The doorway led into a narrow corridor with coursed
rubble walls and a barrel-vault ceiling. Karine led the way
with her flashlight. After about another block we sighted
flashlight beams coming toward us within the confines of
the corridor.

There were three people, in their thirties: two men and
a woman, dressed alike in lumber jackets, dungarees, and

work boots. They were lugging scuba gear with them. One of the men had a wet suit draped over his shoulder. The woman carried flippers and a face mask. The second man had air tanks strapped on his back. They intended to explore the depths of the reservoir and search for its outlet.

"It's very deep," the woman told us. "It could lead someplace interesting nobody has found before."

All three were doctors, just come off duty in Laennec Hospital, which was directly above us at that point. It was their second time down there. They'd learned about this complex from a group of young people who had found their way out via a telephone maintenance manhole that surfaced in a courtyard behind the hospital's emergency building.

I had eight copies of Odile's snapshot with me, and eight more of the boy. I showed one of each to the doctors. They didn't remember having met either Odile or the boy.

"But we have more people joining us later," one of the men told me. "One of them might know these kids."

"Especially Henri Gelfand," the woman added, "if these two are underground enthusiasts. Gelfand has been a troglo for years."

I left them a copy of each picture, with Fritz Donhoff's phone number jotted on the back of one. Fritz was acting as home base for this operation.

Karine and I went on to the end of the corridor. Thick telephone cables and gas pipes crossed the bottom of the manhole the doctors had told us about. Iron rungs led upward. We climbed out, surfacing to find ourselves surrounded by dozens of dark buildings that belonged to Laennec Hospital's block-long complex.

"What I want to try next," I told Karine as we started walking the five blocks back toward Babylon station, "are the places the regulars go into most."

"That's your best chance," Karine agreed. "We could start with the old quarry below Rue St. Jacques. And after that the catacombs near Denfert-Rochereau. They're two of the most popular."

The Friday night traffic had thinned out by that hour. I caught a cab cruising past the Métro station and had it take us to the garage where I kept the Renault 5 I used in Paris. With Karine giving directions, I drove to Rue St. Jacques and parked near a manhole we used to find our way into the first of the underground gathering places she'd suggested.

I met some odd people in both places. And a lot who weren't so odd. Just people. Looking for a way to add a little mystery and adventure to lives that were otherwise too routine. I figured it was a better way than giving up on the world entirely and shooting poison in your veins to forget it existed.

I met several people who recalled having met the boy in the picture I showed them. Like Karine Vidal, however, they knew nothing about him—or Odile.

But it was too early in the search to get discouraged. I left copies of both snapshots in each place we went to. And hoped they'd get shown to somebody who knew one of the people I was hunting. Sooner rather than later.

At midnight we took a break for snacks and drinks at the Coupole in Montparnasse, and I phoned Fritz.

He didn't have anything either. He'd been calling Odile Garnier's apartment once every hour, just in case, without getting a response. His man outside Tony Callega's apartment reported nobody had returned there yet. None of the people among whom the snapshots were being circulated had phoned in so far. Fritz had tried a long-distance call to Eze, but Egon Mulhausser hadn't heard anything new from or about his daughter.

I left the Coupole with Karine, and we headed for some other secret burrows popular with undercity buffs.

At a little before two in the morning we were inside a 1930s bunker underneath the Luxembourg Gardens. It was full of people, noise, and cigarette smoke. They were having a candlelight dancing party: beer, pizzas, and rock music pounding out of a large tape deck. All sorts of people: teenage punks, college kids, well-dressed BCBGs, even several couples in formal evening clothes.

None of them had anything useful about Odile or her boyfriend. I gave out the last copies of their pictures and asked for them to be shown to other troglos over the week-end. That left me with only the originals. I decided to call it quits for the night.

We were invited to join the party. Karine Vidal did, promising to go with me again if I wanted to try once more on Saturday night. I left the way we'd come in, making my stooped way through a low, tortuous tunnel under Rue Vaugirard. It ended at a storm drain. I straightened up, shoved its inlet grill aside, and climbed out into the night shadows behind the darkened Odeon Theater.

There was a young couple in their mid-twenties standing there, smiling at me uncertainly. He was wearing a jacket and pants of soft, expensive leather. She had a fur jacket open over a ballerina's practice outfit: black leotard, tights, and thick striped stockings.

"Is the party over?" the ballerina asked me.

"Going strong," I assured her, and their smiles bright-ened. Without much expectation, I moved them over under a street lamp and showed them the photo of Odile's boy-friend.

They didn't know him. I tried Odile's picture next, with even less hope, but it had become automatic by then.

The guy in leather squinted at the picture and then looked at his companion. "Isn't that the girl we met at Monique Orban's birthday party?"

The ballerina studied the snapshot a bit longer and nod-ded. "Odile . . ." She fished for the last name.

"Garnier," I said, holding down a sudden rise in ten-sion.

"That's right. Odile Garnier."

The guy said, "I don't remember ever hearing her last name."

"Monique told me when I called her last weekend."

I said quietly, "I've been trying to find Odile. Maybe your friend Monique could help."

"Monique's in London this week," the ballerina told me. "That's what I called her about. I knew she was going, and I wanted to borrow her place for a friend who was coming to town for a few days. But she told me she'd already promised to lend it to *her*.'' She gestured at Odile's picture.

I let myself hope. Just a little. "Where is this Monique Orban's apartment?''

"Montmartre, on Rue Fauvet. I don't remember the exact address offhand.''

"Is she in the phone book?''

"Sure.''

I headed for an all-night brasserie on Boulevard St. Germain while they were climbing down into the storm drain.

After getting Monique Orban's address and phone number from the brasserie's phone book I dialed the number and let it ring ten times. No answer. I walked back to my car and drove to her address.

It was in a one-block residential street behind the Montmartre Cemetery. The street was empty at that hour, and none of the building's windows were lighted. A buzzer button clicked open the door to Monique Orban's building. Inside was a short corridor with mailboxes on one wall. I checked them and got the apartment number.

The corridor led to a small, high-walled courtyard. The apartment was on the ground floor. It had a window on the courtyard, covered by locked wooden shutters. To the right was an open entry to a stairway. The door of the apartment was inside the entry.

I decided against knocking. There might be a back way out of the apartment. If Odile was in there, I didn't want to give her time to run out before I could get inside. I put my ear against the door. No sound at all.

The door had a mortise lock. There was just enough light from a bare ceiling bulb halfway up the stairway for me to work. I took out the lock pick I'd brought along.

But I discovered I didn't need it. The door's dead bolt wasn't locked in place. I tried the doorknob and felt the latch bolt slide free.

I kept a hold on the knob with my left hand, not letting the door open. With my right hand, I put the pick away and drew the Beretta from its holster. Holding it ready, I shoved open the door and went in fast, shifting instantly to one side as I slammed the door shut behind me.

Nobody shot at me. There was no sound at all. Just a smell in the darkness. Not overpowering, but definite.

I felt along the wall, found the wall switch, and flicked it on. I was in a neatly furnished living room with a sleeping alcove off to one side.

Maurice was there, holding the same kind of pistol as the last time I'd met him, complete with silencer.

But even the gun didn't make him a threat anymore.

Maurice was the source of the smell.

The smell of death.

⊠ 20 ⊠

HE LAY ON HIS BACK BESIDE A PINEWOOD COFFEE TABLE piled with art books and magazines. His legs were bent together at the knees, both shoes pointing to his left, as though he'd swiveled when had fallen. One arm was folded across his chest. The other was bent outward, clutching the pistol.

His hawklike face was turned to one side, away from the coffee table. He seemed to be looking in wonder at the heavy bronze candlestick lying on the carpet near his head.

One side of Maurice's head had an ugly, indented swelling at the temple, dark from the internal hemorrhage under it. The blow hadn't broken the skin there. The only external bleeding was a little trickle from his nostrils, and that had dried long before.

The candlestick on the floor had a twin. It stood on a rough-hewn wooden beam that formed a mantelpiece over the brick fireplace behind Maurice's corpse.

He had been dead about twenty-four hours, at a guess. Putting his killing sometime during the previous night. The rigor mortis was as solid as if he'd been carved from a single block of wood. Decomposition wasn't as advanced as it would have been if the apartment hadn't been so chilly. The window on the little courtyard wouldn't let in any direct sunlight at any time, even with the shutters open. And the walls were of big blocks of stone. It was the kind of place that would have to be heated from time to time, even in mild weather. And nobody had turned on the electric radiators in the past day. Otherwise Maurice would have smelled worse.

Even so, it wasn't perfume.

I walked through the rest of the apartment via a narrow

corridor. It led past a large kitchen with a dining booth and a good-sized bathroom with the apartment's only other window: a small casement on an alley. At the end of the corridor there was a back door. I opened its chain lock and looked out. The alley behind the apartment cut through the block. At one end, across a dim street with a "oneway" sign, rose the wall of the cemetery.

I went back to the living room and stood beside Maurice, thinking about alternative ways he could have wound up dead on the floor there.

Boyan Traikov and Tony Callega would have split up their search force, to check as many of Odile's contacts as possible in a short time. Maurice had come across somebody who knew Odile and Monique Orban were friendly, as I had. He might have learned that Odile had borrowed this apartment to hide in, and he decided to make himself big by capturing her himself. But more likely he'd come alone without knowing, just to check on whether he could find out something from Monique Orban.

In any case, he had come. After that, the possibilities multiplied. He could have rung the bell, and Odile could have been there and opened the door to him. Or she could have been out, and Maurice might have picked the lock and been waiting inside when she got back. Either way, they'd wound up in here together—and Maurice had gotten careless.

Maybe he hadn't felt he needed to be too careful, with a gun in his hand, against a fairly small teenage girl.

It didn't feel right. Maurice would have to have been *very* careless. He would have had to turn his back on her. Long enough for her to grab that candlestick off the mantel and club him with it before he could turn and shoot her. Why would he turn his back on her? I could think of a number of reasons, but they were all what Fritz would call assumptions. I didn't have anything that changed one of the possibles to a probable.

I got down on my hands and knees and smelled the gun in Maurice's fist. It might or might not have been fired. I

couldn't be sure. And I couldn't get it out of his hand to
make sure without breaking all his fingers.

I stood up and circled the room. There was a small, fresh
hole in the wooden frame of the entrance door. Taking out
my penknife, I probed inside the hole—prying out a small
lead slug. From a 9mm cartridge. The caliber of Maurice's
pistol.

So he had fired. At the door. With Odile behind him.

There were a number of different reasons *that* could have
happened. I didn't dwell on them. It would only be adding
more guesswork to a pile of it that was already too un-
wieldy.

I crouched beside Maurice again and went through his
pockets. His I.D. gave his full name as Maurice Bolec and
his profession as "Travel Guide." Born in Lyons. Current
residence: Cannes—the same address as Tony Callega. So
it was Tony he'd worked for, probably assigned by Tony's
big brother as watchdog and general thug-of-all-work.

He was registered as the owner of the car I'd seen him
drive out of Tony's place. His wallet also contained his
driver's license and an assortment of credit cards. He had
a gold clip with a fat wad of cash, some keys and loose
change, and a spare 9mm ammo magazine for his pistol.

I also found, in a side pocket of his jacket, two black-
and-white snapshots. They were closeups: one of Odile
Garnier, the other of her boyfriend. They were wearing the
same jackets and shirts as in my pictures, and they were
posing against the same stone wall.

That answered a question that had been nagging at me:
why the opposition hadn't bothered to take those Polaroid
snapshots I'd found in Odile's studio in Villefranche. These
were closer and clearer pictures than mine. They'd taken
the *best* ones they'd found—in Villefranche or her Paris
apartment. They'd made fast black-and-white copies of
them, like I had, and had distributed them among their
search force. One of whom was Maurice.

I put the snapshots in my own pocket. There was nothing
else on Maurice to connect him to Odile or her boyfriend.

I replaced the other items in his pockets, smearing each to remove my prints.

Then I searched the apartment. But I didn't find anything I could identify as belonging to Odile Garnier. The clothes in the closets and drawers belonged to a large woman, not someone small and slim. Odile Garnier didn't seem to have left anything of hers behind.

What I decided to do next was worse than dangerous. It was goddamn stupid. But Egon Mulhausser was paying me to protect his daughter, as well as to find her. And as Traikov had pointed out, I did work for money.

First I opened the living room window, leaving the shutters locked. Cool night air drifted in through the shutter's louvers. I went to the bathroom and wound the casement window open. The opening wasn't much; too small for anyone but an infant to climb through. But the cross breeze between it and the living room window would air out the place. Maybe enough, if the apartment's owner took a few more days before returning from London.

Back in the living room, I got out my handkerchief and picked up the bronze candlestick from the floor. It *was* heavy. I wiped it clean and set it on the mantel near its twin. Then I went through the place and wiped everything I had touched, including the outside knob of the entrance door.

Finally I stripped the top cover off the wide bed and draped it over Maurice's body. His feet stuck out of the covering, along with the hand frozen around his gun. Nothing I could do about that. It wasn't total concealment I was after; I was just being squeamish. I wanted as little direct contact between our bodies as I could manage.

Picking him up, with the blanket between us, was an involved operation. So was getting him through the corridor to the rear door. It was like carrying a tree trunk with some of its roots and branches still attached. I was breathing hard and my clothes were soaked with sweat by the time I neared the end of the alley.

There I leaned Maurice against the inside wall, standing

up, and held him that way with one hand while I peeked out. The street between me and Montmartre Cemetery was empty. No cars, no pedestrians. As it should be at three-thirty in the morning. Respectable neighborhood.

I carried his body across the street and halfway down the block. There I finally relinquished my heavy and awk-ward burden, laying it down against the bottom of the cem-etery wall. I would have preferred to dump him inside the cemetery. But I hadn't the strength left to hoist him up and over. I contented myself with tossing his 9mm slug over the wall. Then I hurried back the way I'd come, taking the bed cover with me.

I used my handkerchief again in opening and shutting the back door. The inside breeze I'd started by opening windows at both ends of the apartment was cool and steady. But it still carried the stink of Maurice.

Going to the bedroom alcove, I replaced the cover neatly the way I'd found it. Then I used my handkerchief in going out the front door. After that I walked rapidly to my car and got out of the area.

It was four A.M. when I entered my own apartment. Finding a note from Fritz Donhoff on my living room table didn't startle me. We had keys to each other's apartments, in addition to the secret door we'd rigged between our ad-jacent bedroom closets. Nor was I surprised, at that stage, by his one-word message: "Nothing."

Neither of us had gotten any nearer to finding Odile Gar-nier that night. It was frustrating. But frustration comes with the business. If you can't stand wading through mo-lasses, get out of other people's sticky lives.

I took a very long, hot shower, scrubbing myself with plenty of soap. I shampooed my hair, brushed my teeth, used a file to clean my nails. And still couldn't entirely rid myself of the feeling of contact with Maurice's corpse.

I got in bed, firmly kicked Maurice out of my brain, and was asleep in twenty seconds. But there were dreams. All I could remember later was that in each dream I was drag-ging something monstrous through endless dark tunnels underneath the city. And in one of them the monstrous burden turned its head and grinned at me.

It was noon when the delicious odor of perking coffee woke me. Fritz trudged in from my kitchen, carrying a large cup in one hand and a croissant in his other.

He put them on the chair beside my bed and walked back into the kitchen without a word. Experience had taught him I wasn't worth talking to before I had some breakfast in me.

I ate the croissant and was on my last gulp of coffee when he came back with his own cup. He sat down on the end of my bed and took a sip.

"The name of Odile Garnier's boyfriend," he told me, "is Gilbert Lucca."

⊠ 21 ⊠

THE PHOTOGRAPHS I HAD PUT IN CIRCULATION DURING that long Friday night had reached someone who knew the boy.

"The young man who phoned me," Fritz said, "is named Axel Regis. He's a student at the Ecole des Beaux Arts. So was Gilbert Lucca, last year. He quit because he couldn't earn enough money while devoting so much of his time to school. He supports himself by making imitation art deco jewelry, which he sells to boutiques—here in Paris and elsewhere. But he has continued to belong, with Regis, to an informal group of young troglodytes."

"Does this Regis know where Gilbert Lucca lives?"

"An inexpensive apartment near Porte Saint Denis, behind the Passage du Prado."

"Has he got a phone there?"

"I've called it twice. No answer."

I got off the bed and went to the bathroom. While I took a fast shower Fritz leaned against the side of the open door and told me more.

"Regis recognized the picture of Odile Garnier, too. I told him her father's not well and is anxious to locate her. But Regis doesn't know anything at all about her except her first name—and he has a feeling she and Gilbert Lucca are very much in love. Regis only met her once. Gilbert Lucca brought her along with him the first time their group explored that place you went to last night—near the Babylon Métro. That was back in March."

"The postcard Odile got was sent last month," I said as I toweled myself dry. "The tenth of April."

"The group went down there a second time last month. On the the third Friday in April. Their group meets once each month for their explorations. Always on the third Friday, at ten at night. But they never send cards like that. They phone each other. And Regis is sure nobody in the group knows her address—here or in Villefranche.''

'' "Except Gilbert Lucca.''

"Yes. The card being signed with a heart seems to confirm that he was the one who sent it. To remind her of that rendezvous. Though, as a matter of fact, neither he nor Odile showed up there that time. Regis doesn't know why.''

"Does he have *anything* else on either of them?''

"Only a bit of background on Gilbert Lucca,'' Fritz told me. "By the way, if you're hungry, I've left the makings of an omelette in your kitchen. Breakfast for you, lunch for me.''

I put on bathrobe and slippers, took my empty cup into the kitchen, and refilled it from the pot Fritz had prepared. He sat down at the table with his own cup but refused a refill. I downed some of my second cup, took a bite out of the fresh baguette he'd left on the counter, and began whipping together the omelette. Six eggs, a good amount of ham and grated cheese, a dash of milk, and a generous sprinkling of herbs. While I worked Fritz told me what little Regis knew of Gilbert Lucca's background.

He'd been born somewhere in the provinces, the son of Italian immigrants. His father had died when Gilbert Lucca was very young, and his mother a few years ago. He'd moved to Paris shortly after that. By then he'd already begun earning money with his jewelry. Enough to pay for his first year at the Beaux Arts. But his income wasn't steady enough for him to continue in the school—although, according to Regis, the work he did was unusually good. And that was all Regis had been able to give Fritz. He and Gilbert Lucca were not close, just friendly acquaintances.

The omelette was ready by then. I divided it between two plates and put the plates on the table with the baguette and a pot of butter. "Records here in town might have something useful on him,'' I said as we ate.

"I've already checked around for that," Fritz said. *"Naturally."*

"Naturally," I agreed dryly. "I apologize for implying you needed me to suggest it."

"You are forgiven," Fritz said blandly. "Gilbert Lucca is registered as both 'Student' and 'Artisan.' He has never had a problem with the law. The only year he earned enough to pay taxes was the year he attended the Beaux Arts. Judging by what that left of his income, I understand his not being able to afford a second year at the school. And he owns a second-hand van. One of those little Fiat *camionnettes.*"

He pushed a slip of paper with its license number across to me. "Also," he added, "Gilbert Lucca was born in Menton."

I got one of those shivery feelings that hit you sometimes—when an investigation suddenly starts turning you back toward the point you started from.

"Menton," I said, "is only forty minutes from Villefranche along the Lower Corniche. Even by bus. Five minutes more to Nice."

"Which *may* be significant," Fritz acknowledged. "So I made a call to one of my police contacts down there."

"Naturally."

Fritz smiled benignly. "My contact is with the *gendarmerie* in Menton. He will call me back soon, after making a thorough check on Gilbet Lucca in the files there and at the central records office in Nice."

I finished my breakfast slowly, considering what could be made of the proximity of Menton—where Gilbert Lucca was born—to the studio of Odile's aunt in Villefranche. The possibility that Odile and Gilbert had known each other before he'd moved to Paris.

"Is that all you've got for me?" I asked Fritz. "I don't want to ask any more questions you might regard as insulting."

"I did accept your apology, my boy. Yes, that's all."

I told him about my long night—including what I'd found

and done at the apartment Odile had borrowed from her absent friend.

He pursed his lips in a soundless whistle, gazing at me with a certain amount of wonder. "The tightrope you are walking," he said, "is becoming dangerously frayed."

"You can quit now, if you're worried about taking the tumble with me."

"I am worried," Fritz said, without sounding it. "But more interested in seeing how it turns out. And you'll need all the help you can get, if anyone discovers you've distorted murder evidence."

"If they kick me out of France, I'll just have to go back to work in America. Maybe that's where I belong, anyway."

"But maybe *they* won't have you, either."

That was not unlikely.

"Also," Fritz said, "you just may have misinterpreted what you found in that apartment. It's possible someone else killed Maurice. Even possible that Odile doesn't know of it."

"You don't really believe that."

"No. But it is not entirely unlikely. She *could* be back there now, wondering if she forgot to close those windows."

I got up abruptly and dialed the number of the apartment Odile had borrowed from Monique Orban. There was no answer. I put down the phone and frowned at Fritz. "You're wrong."

"Probably. It was merely a stray thought."

I cleared my nerves of his stray thought and asked him, "How long ago was your last call to Gilbert Lucca's place?"

"Just before I woke you." Fritz gave me the phone number.

I tried it. Still no response there. I went to my jacket and took out the two snapshots I'd lifted from Maurice.

Fritz regarded them and nodded. "These *are* better than the ones we have. We should get some quick copies made at the camera shop down the street."

I asked if he would take care of that. He said he would. He didn't ask what I would be doing because he already knew.

I shaved and dressed, took Gilbert Lucca's address, and went to see what I could find there.

⊠ 22 ⊠

No Parisian BCBG would be caught dead buying anything in the Passage du Prado.

It's not on a par with such fashionable shopping arcades as the Passage des Princes and the Galerie Vivienne. The cluttered shops under its long, dark glass roof lean heavily toward cheap imports from rock-bottom countries, offered at bargain basement prices. The Prado belongs where it is, in the congested quarter just above the Porte Saint Denis. A neighborhood of people who make do by counting every franc, very carefully.

The way up to Gilbert Lucca's place was a sagging stairway recessed between a Turkish café and a Pakistani clothing and cosmetics shop. I climbed to the third floor and turned into a wide, high-ceilinged hallway that had been recently whitewashed.

There was an open window on one side that looked down on the cracked, soot-covered roof of the Passage du Prado. Between the high building walls, rising on either side, it looked like a river of mud flowing through the bottom of a straight, narrow canyon. The river seemed to be in movement—the illusion caused by the crowds walking past the lighted shops underneath it.

On the other side of the hallway were numbered apartment doors. Gilbert Lucca's was number eight. I knocked, waited, and then inserted my pick into the lock's keyhold. Half a minute's work and I had the tumblers turned. I slid my right hand under my jacket, gripped the Beretta, and went in.

The apartment was a large single room with a ceiling as high as the hallway's. I could see every part of it from the doorway. It was empty. I shut and relocked the door behind me.

Gilbert Lucca's place was bigger and better than what most students from the provinces find when they move to Paris to attend the universities. It even had its own little bathroom. A lot of the college students get by with communal toilets out in the hall. And without windows. This room had two—one on the street side, another looking over the top of the glass roof of the passage at a section of blank wall.

Another interloper had been there before me. The damage was the same as that at Odile's studio in Villefrance and at her Paris apartment. An easy chair and the mattress of the wide brass bed had been gutted. Furniture was overturned and broken open. The contents of cardboard boxes containing materials for Gilbert's jewelry had been dumped on the linoleum floor: colored bits of glass and beads, wire and patterned stones, cutouts from sheets of metal.

The emptied boxes had been pulled from a section of built-in shelves. Among them were a few completed samples of Gilbert Lucca's jewelry. I picked up a couple of them. An earring, fashioned out of a 1920s ornamental button. A pendant made from beads, strung together so their delicate colors were skillfully integrated. Regis was right: superb craftsmanship with inexpensive materials.

I put them on a shelf and began a methodical prowl of the room.

I found three Polaroid snapshots. One of Odile, a second of her with Gilbert Lucca, a third of him with another man. They were wearing the same outfits as in the two pictures I'd found in Villefranche. In the shot of Odile alone she was standing in front of the same stone wall.

What I didn't find were certain items that were conspicuous by their absence. There was no address book, no letters, nothing to tell me who his friends or business contacts were. No copies of sales slips. No record of checks he'd received. No list of boutiques to which he sold his work.

Even a very small one-man business has to keep books—some record of sales and expenses and customers.

The reason they were missing wasn't hard to figure. If *I'd* found them first, Fritz and I would have used them to contact Gilbert Lucca's clients, in Paris and elsewhere. Any of whom might know something recent about him that could lead to Odile Garnier.

Getting in touch with all of them and questioning each one would have been a very time-consuming job for just the two of us. But it wouldn't take as long with all the people Didier Sabarly and Fulvio Callega could put on it.

That was how Maurice had gotten to Monique Orban's place before me. And how they'd gotten to this apartment before I had. They'd started with people Tony Callega knew among Odile's friends and contacts—and put a lot of manpower into following all the connections from those. Somewhere along one of those lines they'd hit someone who knew about her relationship with Gilbert Lucca.

But they'd missed something. They hadn't seen what I saw in two of the Polaroids, or they wouldn't have left them behind for me to find.

I studied them again. Seen together, their backgrounds were unmistakable. It helped that Fritz had just told me where Gilbert Lucca was from. But there was no way I could have missed recognizing it even without that. Menton, the last town on the French Riviera before the Italian border, was less than a half hour's drive from my house. I'd been there often enough. The thieves who'd taken the other items obviously hadn't.

In the shot of Odile and Gilbert Lucca together, they were sitting at the top of a wide, cobbled stairway with an orange-colored wall behind them. The cobbles, some dark and some light, were arranged to form graceful patterns. In the oldest section of Menton there was a stairway like that, leading down from the orange-walled church of Saint Michel.

The other picture was of Gilbert Lucca and a fat young man wearing a red apron, standing with their arms around each other's shoulders, grinning. They were outside a bistro with a red awning and red shade umbrellas over the terrace tables. To one side was a stone archway with a tiled roof, and through the arch could be seen a parking lot with a palm tree.

Menton's Place aux Herbes had an archway like that, separating it from the parking area. It also had a bistro whose awning, umbrellas, and waiters' aprons were all red. I probed my memory until I came up with the bistro's name: *Le Lido*.

Gilbert Lucca's phone was still working. I phoned Fritz Donhoff. "Has your friend in Menton called back yet?"

"Fifteen minutes ago. With only routine background, I'm sorry to say. Nothing exciting. Gilbert Lucca's parents were originally from Naples. His father was a commercial fisherman who was drowned in a storm when the boy was five. His mother worked as a seamstress until her death, from an illness, when he was eighteen. He is twenty-one now, and he started adding to his mother's small income by making jewelry when he was fifteen. He began selling it at the flea market in Menton. He left Menton for Paris three years ago—and there's nothing further on record about him down there after that."

"That flea market he used for selling his work," I told Fritz, "is only in Menton one day each week. The other days it moves to other towns. A different one each day. Every Sunday it's in Villefranche."

"Ah," Fritz said, "that I didn't know. It does strengthen the possibility he and the girl met well before his move to Paris. *If* he was showing his wares in Villefranche at some time when Odile was down there with her aunt."

"When that flea market is in Menton," I said, "it's held on the Place aux Herbes. Which has a bistro called the Lido. One of the waiters there might be an old friend of Gilbert Lucca." I explained about the snapshot.

Fritz agreed it was worth another phone call to his gendarmerie contact in Menton. "I'll ask him to check with the people in the Lido."

"I'll be back with you in about twenty minutes." I hung up the phone and left Gilbert Lucca's apartment.

As I stepped out into the hallway I caught a flash of movement: a man disappearing quickly down the stairway before I could see his face. All I got was an impression of someone not too tall and fairly thin in a gray suit and cloth cap.

I strolled along the hallway and took my time going down the stairway into the Passage du Prado.

A thin man in a gray suit and cap stood at the bottom with his back to me, apparantly absorbed in the articles displayed in the Pakistani shop. I'd seen him before. When I'd gone up the stairs he'd been sitting at a window table inside the Turkish café.

I walked out of the passage and along the crowded pavement to my Renault, parked half a block away. I didn't look back until I could do so without it being obvious, while I was unlocking my car.

The thin man in gray had stopped beside a white four-door Lada and bent to speak to someone inside it. The Lada was eight cars back from mine, parked facing the same direction.

I got into the Renault, started it, and kept an eye on my rearview mirror while I did some tight maneuvering to get free of the cars parked in front and back of mine. As I drove away the thin man walked back to the Passage du Prado.

The Lada came after me.

⊠ **23** ⊠

I DROVE ACROSS THE CITY TO BABYLON. THE WHITE LADA stayed about half a block behind me the whole way. Too far back for me to make out the face of the man driving it. But the important thing I did see: He was alone.

Swinging past the Métro station, I drove into the entrance of the underground parking garage across from the Bon Marché. I stopped at the barrier and pressed the meter button. It fed me a timed parking stub and raised the striped yellow-and-black boom. I drove through and down the spiral ramp.

I went all the way down. To the fifth level, where the ramp ended. Taking a flat flashlight from the glove compartment, I walked between other parked cars to the ladder that led down to the partially excavated sixth level. I'd counted on none of the construction crew being at work on a Saturday. None was there.

The white Lada came around the bottom of the ramp. The instant I was sure the driver had seen me, I switched on my flashlight and went down the ladder. From the foot of it there was nowhere to go except through the low tunnel. I went to my hands and knees and crawled into it. The last time, with Karine leading, I hadn't known what was ahead. This time I did.

I reached the other end of the crawl space, where it opened into the abandoned military shelter. My tail hadn't come into the tunnel behind me yet. I stretched to the right of its opening and put the flash on the ground, its beam pointed away from the tunnel. Then I moved to my left and stood up near that side of the tunnel, drawing my Beretta from its holster. I waited, listening to the faint scraping noises of his crawling approach.

His fist poked through first, holding a revolver. Even with the flashlight beam aimed in the opposite direction, there was enough light from it to see the short, thick barrel. A .45. Then he pushed his head out of the low opening, cautiously, turning both his face and gun toward where I'd put the flashlight.

I bent down and stuck the muzzle of my Beretta in his ear. The shock made his head jerk a fraction. Then he froze in position.

"Put it down," I said thinly.

He placed the revolver on the concrete floor, spread his fingers, and raised them well away from it. "Don't get nervous," he whispered. "I'm no trouble."

"I've got no reason to be nervous," I told him unpleasantly. "You're the one with a gun in your ear." I picked up his snub-nosed revolver and stuck it in my belt. "Now crawl all the way out and stand up."

As he crawled into the bunker I withdrew my gun from his ear and moved back a step. When he got to his feet and turned to face me I was holding the Beretta level with his stomach.

It was a fairly large stomach, but a lot of that was still heavy muscle that went with the rest of his squat, powerful build. He had a strong-boned face that had taken a lot of punishment in its time without losing any of its menace. At the moment, the menace was confined to the broken sculpture of his features. His expression was apprehensive.

He raised his hands over his head without being asked to. "No reason to get rough," he whispered. "All I did was follow you, nothing else."

There had to be something wrong with his vocal chords. This deep under the streets there was no reason to whisper. Nobody would have heard if we'd yelled at the top of our lungs.

I said, "You followed me with a gun. You were going to use it to ask me some questions. And then kill me."

"No," he said, "I'm not a shooter. The gun's just insurance."

"Your policy just ran out," I told him. "Move to the middle of the room. Five steps, no more."

He measured off five steps exactly, backing up, afraid to take his eyes off me and the gun in my hand. I picked up the flashlight with my free hand. "Go to that metal partition against the wall," I ordered. "Face it and put your hands against it, shoulder level."

I kept the flashlight and Beretta on him as I followed him to the partition and watched him obey the order. "Back your feet toward me and spread them." He did. "Further," I snapped. He did that, too. Now he was stretched out with all his weight on his hands. I holstered the Beretta and patted him down. No other gun. I went through his pockets.

According to his ID, he was Christophe Bucher, thirty-four years old, born in Strasbourg, now resident in Paris, profession: chauffeur. I found two snapshots, the same ones of Odile and Gilbert Lucca. I put them in my pocket, found a switchblade knife, and stuck that in my pocket, too. The next thing I found was a small address book.

I went through it quickly, looking first under "S". No Didier Sabarly. No Callega, neither Tony nor Fulvio. I tried "T". Boyan Traikov was there: a phone number, but no address. No other names that meant anything to me. I pocketed the little book for possible future reference and moved back a step, drawing the Beretta again.

Bucher asked, "Can I straighten up now? My arms are starting to hurt."

"Nothing's going to hurt you much longer if I don't get some fast and straight answers. Who do you work for?"

"Anybody that pays us."

"*Us* being you and your partner back there at the Passage du Prado."

"That's right. We'd work for *you* if you hired us to. So no reason for you to—"

"What's your partner's name?"

"Rheims. Alain Rheims."

It was one of the names in his little book. "And right

now you're working for Boyan Traikov and Tony Callega.''

He hesitated just a bit. "No, a guy named Planel. Robert Planel."

That *wasn't* in his little book. I let it pass for the moment. "Are you the ones who searched Gilbert Lucca's place?"

"No, we were never inside there."

It was possible that their assignment had followed the search. "What were you supposed to do there outside his place?"

"Just watch it. In case Lucca or the girl showed up there. Or if somebody else came there, one of us was supposed to follow him. Like I did with you. Just to find out where you went. Nothing else, no rough stuff."

"If Lucca or the girl came back there," I said, "then what?"

"Call this guy and let him know, that's all."

"Planel?"

"Planel, sure."

"Give me his phone number."

Bucher told me a number.

I said, "Nobody's ever going to know what you tell me down here. But lie to me again and nobody will know *anything* about you again, ever."

"I don't *know* the number!" Bucher's whisper had become strained. "My partner's got it. Rheims has it."

I sighed and said, "You can straighten up now."

He looked surprised as he did so, rubbing his aching biceps and forearms.

"Now we take a walk," I told him, and I gestured at the doorway on the other side of the bunker. "You first."

With apparent docility, Bucher walked ahead of me into the passage. I followed two steps behind. When we reached the place where the passage forked I directed him to the left-hand passage. As we neared the point where it ended at the subterranean reservoir he began to shorten his steps. Just a little, so I'd be closer behind him. I didn't say anything. What he had in mind could establish a better relationship between us. From my viewpoint.

The instant we stepped out of the end of the passage he sidestepped and spun around to grab my gun arm. Since I'd been waiting for it, I had time to shoot him exactly where I wanted to. His reaching hand.

Bucher squealed, stumbled backward, and fell. He screamed again when his wounded hand struck the rough rock beside the black pool. He rolled, and his legs slid into the water. I think the water's being there shocked him as much as the agony in his smashed hand. He yanked his dripping legs out and sat up abruptly, holding his hurt hand with his other and cradling it between his chest and upraised knees.

The wound would have been worse if I'd shot him with his own .45. But even a 9mm bullet going through the palm of a hand doesn't leave many bones unsplintered.

Bucher looked around fearfully at the black surface of the water and the crumbling arches. His whisper was wracked with pain. "What *is* this place?"

"You wanted to know where I was going. This is it. That water is deep. It runs under the rock and keeps going underneath the city for miles. Nobody knows where. And nobody will ever find your body."

I felt the muscles of my face stretching so tight it almost hurt. A kind of smile. I'd been told it wasn't a joy to look at.

His whisper became clogged with terror. "I didn't *do* anything to you!"

I took aim at the spot between his eyes. "The next time you lie to me I'm going to shoot you in the head and dump you in there," I said tonelessly. "Who are you working for?"

Bucher was in no shape by then to call my bluff. He was bleeding and hurt and scared. "Boyan Traikov," he told me.

That felt right. Bucher was too small to deal with Didier Sabarly directly. "What number were you supposed to call him at, if Gilbert Lucca or the girl showed up?"

He rattled off a number. I looked up Traikov in Bucher's little book. It was Traikov's number—at his second residence, the one Fritz hadn't been able to locate. Bucher's knowing the number by heart meant he worked for Boyan Traikov with some regularity.

I said, "He's sticking to his place while he waits for the call?"

"Not just from us. He's got a lot of other people out looking for those two kids." Bucher moaned softly, bending his head over the injured hand as though he wanted to kiss it.

"Is Tony Callega still with him?"

"Not anymore. He went back south to take care of some other business."

"What kind of business?"

"I don't know. . . . Jesus, my hand is—"

"Finding the girl? Or getting another supply of heroin for Didier Sabarly?"

"I don't *know*!"

I believed him. And he only had two other items of any interest to me.

One: Bucher and his partner had been assigned to watch Gilbert Lucca's place early that morning. By which time it must have been searched. That meant Gilbert Lucca had been away from his place since before then. It didn't tell me whether Odile was with him or not.

Two: One of the opposition's searchers had disappeared two nights ago. Bucher didn't know which one. I figured that had to be Maurice.

I dropped Bucher's revolver into the dark pool. "You can dive for that if you want. But don't leave here for at least fifteen minutes." I left him hunched beside the water, fastening his necktie around his wrist as a tourniquet.

"What took you so long?" Fritz asked when I entered his apartment.

I told him and gave him Bucher's address book.

He looked through it and said, "It *may* prove of some use—if not on this assignment, perhaps in some future one." Fritz kept a stock of items like it, acquired over the years by various means. He regarded me dubiously. "But other than this, I wouldn't say you learned enough to justify all that effort."

"Not much," I agreed. "But I couldn't know that before I tried it. What did you get from Menton?"

"The waiter with Gilbert Lucca in that snapshot," he told me, "is Dominique Veran. He's known Gilbert since he was a kid. And he knows our Odile, by name. Gilbert introduced her to him, as his girlfriend, the day those pictures were taken. During a visit Odile and Gilbert paid to Menton this February."

Fritz paused. But I'd detected the faint undercurrent in his tone, so I kept silent and waited until he answered the question I hadn't asked.

"The last time Dominique Veran saw them down there was yesterday."

⊠ **24** ⊠

LATE THAT AFTERNOON I WAS BACK ON THE CÔTE D'AZUR.

The newspaper I'd bought before catching the flight from Paris carried a story about the finding of Maurice's body. A small item, on an inside page. The police reported that he was known to be a member of the underworld *milieu* in southern France. Since the gun found in his hand had been fired, it was probable he had been killed during a fight with a rival gang in Paris. Nothing to worry normal, peaceful citizens. I breathed easier, a normal, peaceful citizen.

I'd left my Peugeot in the parking garage under the airport terminal when I'd flown up to Paris. Before driving it out I got the H&K from its hiding place and holstered it under my Levi jacket. Then I drove east along the coast road.

There were a good three hours of daylight left. But the sun was becoming obscured by a cloud cover like the one over Paris. Over the sea, however, it had its own kind of beauty. Shafts of sunlight stabbed through holes in the clouds and created bright gold disks on the slate-gray surface of the Mediterranean. There was a fairly strong breeze, but it lacked the chill of the north. Sailboats and windsurfers were out there taking advantage of it. The water was too placid for any storm to be brewing.

I drove past my house without stopping and went on to Menton.

Coming from that direction, you first enter its modern section, stretching for about a mile along the shore from Cap Martin to the old fishing port. Beyond that the casbah-like older part of town rises across a slope surrounding the multicolored steeple of Saint Michel.

The Place aux Herbes is tucked between the old and new

sections, next to the covered market near the port. Dominique Veran, the waiter in the snapshot with Gilbert Lucca, wasn't there when I arrived. He'd just finished his day's work and had gone down for a swim. I strolled the long pebble beach, looking for him.

The air and sea were warm enough for the beach to still be crowded, in spite of the clouds. But it wasn't the St. Tropez sort of beach crowd. St. Tropez and Menton are at opposite ends of the Rivera, and they are opposite in most other ways. St. Tropez is frenetic and hip; Menton quiet and conservative, with a large enclave of elderly retired people. You don't see any full nudity on its beaches, even among the young set. Topless has made inroads but still draws stares. Some find Menton boring, others regard it as restful—depends what you're looking for.

Dominique Veran was coming out of the gentle surf when I spotted him. He wasn't difficult to spot. In his early twenties, he had a tubby body and a cheerful face like a full moon, with skin that had the stretched shine of an overinflated balloon. While he washed off the sea salt at one of the showers under the Promenade du Soleil I explained about trying to find Odile Garnier for her ill and anxious father.

He was eager to be helpful but had no idea where Odile and Gilbert Lucca were. Nor even whether they were staying in the Menton area or had just been passing through. All he'd seen of them was a brief glimpse.

"I was taking a walk during my lunch break yesterday," he explained, "and I saw Gi-Gi's *camionnette* stopped for a traffic light. Gi-Gi—that's what we all called Gilbert in school. He was behind the wheel and Odile was sitting beside him. They didn't see me. I hurried over, but I'm not the fastest walker in the world. By the time I got there the light had changed, and they were driving off."

"You're sure it was Odile with him."

"Sure." Dominique grinned. "I couldn't miss *that* face. That's one really pretty girl he finally got himself. And just what he needs. Gi-Gi was always too serious. No time for anything outside of making a living and building himself a solid business. Odile's full of life and fun. She perks him up.''

"How well did you get to know her when they were down here in February?" I asked as I walked him back to his beach bag.

He picked up his towel and began drying himself. "I only met her the couple times they dropped into the Lido when I was there."

"But you like her."

"Hard not to. A girl like that. Pretty, full of life, *and* with a warm heart. Gi-Gi hit lucky."

"Did she seem worried about anything?"

The question surprised him. "Not that I noticed."

"Where did they stay when they were here in February?"

"With Denis Boyer. He was one of our classmates, too. And he's got a spare room in his apartment. His wife left him and went back to her parents. Took their baby with her. Denis was definitely *not* lucky in his choice."

Dominique Veran gave me the names of some other friends of Gilbert. He only knew a couple of their addresses offhand. I jotted down the names, thanked him, and went back up to the Lido to check the names in its phone book.

Denis Boyer and two of the other names were listed. The rest apparently didn't have phones. I called Denis Boyer first and got him in. But Gilbert and Odile weren't staying with him this time. He didn't even know they were back in the area. The only other help he was able to give me were the addresses of those friends of Gilbert's not listed in the phone book—by looking them up in his personal address book.

I called the other two who had phones but got no answer at either number. Then I began hiking around to the other adresses. By nine that night I'd talked to several of Gilbert's friends in person and gotten one of the other two on the phone. None of them had seen Gilbert and Odile since February, and none had anything much to tell me. Except

for an interesting pattern of disparate opinions of Gilbert's
girlfriend.

Dominique Veran had told me Odile was a lively girl
full of good humor. Another of Gilbert's friends described
her as very quiet and introverted. A third said she was
extremely tense, her nerves jumpy, her temper edgy. Denis
Boyer, the one they'd stayed with in February, had found
her moods to be unpredictable: sometimes up, other times
way down. He couldn't come up with any reason for her
drastic shifts.

I could. It would fit the uncontrollable phases experienced in heroin addiction. Anyone deeply hooked rides an
emotional and physical roller coaster. A fix produces a rush
of euphoria. When the high diminishes the result is sleep-
iness, lethargy, and finally depression. As the need for the
next fix builds the nervous system begins to scream for it,
painfully and insistently, blocking out any other concern.

A pattern that sounded very much like what I was being
told about Odile Garnier.

I tried the remaining phone number again. It belonged
to Paul Delouette, a former schoolmate of Gilbert Lucca.
He was now a clerk in a local bank. His apartment was in
Carnolès, at the western end of Menton's modern section.
But he still wasn't home.

Another of Gilbert's friends whom I hadn't found at
home worked as a bartender not far from Delouette's address. In the Piccadilly: a large brasserie with a relaxed
atmosphere and the best inexpensive food in town, which
made it Menton's favorite hangout for the young crowd.

I drove there and had a talk with the bartender. He was
slim and handsome, and he'd been working there ever since
I'd first begun dropping in for an occasional meal or drink.
But this was the first time I'd ever heard his last name. I'd
always known him as Freddie, and he always called me by
my first name. It was that kind of place.

Freddie wanted to be helpful, but he couldn't tell me
anything at all, except that Gilbert and Odile had been there
for dinner twice in February, not at all since then. His

opinion of Odile: "Gorgeous and good-natured, and in love with Gi-Gi—what more could a man ask for?"

I asked him about the address of the bank clerk, Paul Delouette, because it was in one of the newer streets I didn't know, recently built at that end of town. Freddie told me it was a few blocks away, off Rue Morillot. "But if Paul isn't answering his phone, you might as well wait for him here. He drops in every Saturday night."

With a wave of his hand that indicated the large proportion of female clientele in the brasserie, he added with an indulgent smile, "Looking to pick up a girl, naturally. Paul's a bachelor." Freddie himself looked twenty-five but was thirty-six, with a wife and three children.

It was past my dinnertime by then anyway. I settled at one of the few unoccupied tables and ordered the Piccadilly's most popular meal: roast gigot with spaghetti Bolognese and green salad. Some of the tables near me were taken by young couples, but most were taken by groups of boys or groups of girls, with a certain amount of joking chatter between the two. And an occasional boy shifting from his group for closer conversation with one of the girls. Paul Delouette wasn't the only young man who found the Piccadilly a good place to meet girls.

You could tell the local boys from the ones doing their military service at the fort on the upper edge of town. The draftees were out of uniform but had short haircuts. They were there hoping to pick up a date for the night, and the girls were there hoping to be picked up by someone new and interesting.

It wasn't like what went on around St. Tropez. These were local girls, and they weren't after a fast and furious taste of the rich life. They were interested in connecting with a young man of their own economic and social level, someone who might turn out to be a steady boyfriend and potential husband.

It worked out that way surprisingly often. A lot of the soldiers returned after their service was finished and settled down to jobs and marriage at that end of the Côte d'Azur.

I was having an additional glass of wine after my meal

when I saw Freddie point me out to a stocky young guy who was going prematurely bald. He came over with a drink and introduced himself: Paul Delouette, the bank clerk friend of Gilbert Lucca.

I invited him to sit down. He cast a thoughtful eye at six girls gathered around a nearby table as he did so. Then he said, before I could ask him anything, "If you're looking for Gilbert, he's not around here. Not now. He drove over to Italy yesterday."

🔯 **25** 🔯

"WHERE IN ITALY?"

"That I don't know," Delouette said. "Just visiting some Italian boutiques that buy his work. Gilbert has some regular customers over there, scattered between the frontier and Rome. He's a good salesman, you know. And his Italian is perfect, because that's where his parents came from."

"You're *sure* about this. He's in Italy now."

Delouette nodded. "He came into the bank yesterday afternoon to buy gas coupons for the trip."

Gasoline prices in Italy are higher than in France. But people traveling to Italy can purchase coupons before crossing the border, entitling them to gas at French rates.

"Gilbert said he was running short of cash," Delouette added. "So he told me was going over there for a few days with a new stock of his jewelry, to try to make some sales."

"Did he take Odile Garnier with him?"

Delouette didn't know her name. I showed him her picture. He said, "Oh, his girlfriend. I met her once, when they were down here together in February. But I don't know if he had her with him this time. I didn't see her, and he didn't mention it."

But Dominique Veran *had* seen them together. Anyway, Gilbert Lucca remained my best lead to Odile. And he was now in Italy—somewhere.

I got some five-franc pieces from Freddie, put them into the pay phone at the rear of the Piccadilly, and called Fritz.

I explained the situation and asked him, "That Carabinieri major you know in Milan—does he still owe you a favor?"

"Romano Delisio. Yes, he does. And there is Colonel Diego Bandini, of the Carabinieri in Rome, who owes me another. I imagine I can persuade both of them to circulate official inquiries about Gilbert Lucca's whereabouts in Italy. That *is* what you have in mind, I suppose."

"You suppose correctly," I told him. "*Naturally.*" Italy strictly requires that hotels—and every other kind of establishment taking in guests—register their patrons' identity papers and promptly pass the information on to the local police. Since the rise of terrorism in that country, the regulation has been enforced more stringently than ever.

"At this time of night," Fritz pointed out, "I'll probably have to contact Delisio and Bandini at their homes. Then we have the rest of Saturday night ahead of us, and tomorrow is Sunday. A difficult time to get prompt responses from local police."

"Ask you Carabinieri officers to slap an extremely urgent tag on their inquiries," I said. "And I do realize that means we'll owe *them* a large favor."

"Which they will collect, eventually. Perhaps with requests that will be most uncomfortable for us."

"I don't see any alternative, Fritz."

"Nor do I, unfortunately. Even so, you can't expect an answer before sometime tomorrow—or Monday. I suggest you go home and get a sound night's sleep. Taking proper precautions, of course."

Which was what I did. When you're on an investigation it's a good idea to pack in as much sleep as possible whenever the opportunity presents itself. You never know when you'll have to go two or three days without any.

I approached my house with care, gun in hand. After a wary reconnaissance around the exterior in the dark I let myself in by the patio door even more cautiously. None of the opposition lay in wait for me. I checked every room to make sure. Then I relocked the patio door and switched on the burglar alarms for the doors and windows. Nobody was going to get in that night without my waking in time.

Nobody tried. I guessed that meant the opposition couldn't spare anyone to flick me out of the race. All their manpower would be focused on hunting for Odile Garnier.

I fervently hoped they hadn't found out yet that Gilbert Lucca had driven down here with her—and was now across the border in Italy.

I slept late Sunday morning. When I got up I took the gun from under my pillow and carried it into the bathroom, leaving it on top of the toilet tank while I had my shower. Then I took it into the kitchen and made myself breakfast. Normally I prefer to go out to eat when there's nobody home with me. But I was waiting for that phone call.

The clouds had drifted away during the night. The sea below was tempting. But it's impractical to take a gun for a swim. Instead I worked off the tension of waiting with some strenuous garden preparations.

I'd collected a pile of sizable rocks beside the toolshed the week before. The rest of that morning I spent hauling them, one by one, down to the slope just below one side of my patio, where I planned to make a narrow terrace for flowering shrubs.

One advantage to doing that particular job, at that particular time, was the unobstructed view I got of every approach to the house. It was hot in the sun, and I worked stripped down to sneakers, old tennis shorts, and my shoulder holster. Wearing a gun while gardening is not too comfortable, but it was soothing for the nerves, under the circumstances—somewhat like a Linus blanket.

I got a pickax and shovel from the shed and devoted an hour to digging the trench. Then I manhandled the rocks into a row inside it to hold the soil in place and dumped dirt back in, tamping it down until each rock was securely anchored.

By then I was grimy, drenched with perspiration, and hungry. Still no phone call. I took another shower and made myself lunch. After I'd eaten I made a couple calls of my own. Not to Fritz. When he had anything to tell he would call me.

My first call was to St. Roch Hospital in Nice. I asked for Laurent Soumagnac's room. The last time I'd called there I'd gotten a nurse. This time he answered himself.

His voice was cheerful and strong. "They're letting me go home tomorrow. Better get in practice, Pierre-Ange. I'll be whipping you at flipper again soon."

"According to my count," I told him, "I'm some twenty games ahead of you at this point."

"The devil you are. I've been beating you two games to one for over a month."

I hung up, relieved about his condition and spirits, and decided this was my day for phoning hospitals. The second was the clinic in London. After being paged Arlette came on the line. Her father had come through the stomach operation with surprising strength, considering his age, she told me. "If he continues to hold up like he is, I'll be able to leave him for a while and get back to work."

"Give him my best," I said, not totally insincerely.

"I will. By the way, your mother flew over from Paris to lend him some moral support before and after the operation. She still doesn't forget he saved her life, after all these years. A remarkable woman."

"Remarkable."

"She was somewhat surprised that you weren't here, too." Arlette said. "I explained to your mother about your being too involved right now with an important case."

"Thank you. And give Babette my regards."

"I'll give her your *love*," Arlette said. She understood, as well as Fritz did, the vagaries of the emotional weather between Babette and me.

I went back outside to do some more work on the new terrace. When I was halfway across the patio the phone rang. I returned to the living room and picked it up. Fritz Donhoff was on the line.

"Gilbert Lucca was registered at an inexpensive *pensione* in Genoa last night," he told me. "Before he left there this morning he phoned ahead and reserved a room at a *pensione* in Florence for tonight." He gave me its name.

"Single reservation," I asked him, "or for two?"

"Single. She's not with him."

I cursed softly as I hung up. It wasn't good. But I didn't have anything else. Just Gilbert Lucca.

I switched on my answering machine. My overnight bag was already packed for the drive into Italy. I picked it up and was at the door with it when the phone rang again. I hesitated. The machine wouldn't take over until after the third ring. On the second I went back, picked up the phone, and switched off the machine.

It was Egon Mulhausser calling.

"My daughter—" he started to say, and then his voice choked up. He sounded very near to crying.

"I'm getting closer to her," I told him quickly, to calm him. It might not even be a lie—but it wasn't something I would have put a heavy bet on.

"She called me," he said thickly.

That brought me to instant attention. "When?"

"Sometime this morning—while I was at the restaurant. She phoned our house. Probably because she didn't want to give *me* a chance to say anything. She left a message for me on the answering machine. I just found it when I took an early break from our lunchtime business."

"Where did she call from?"

"I don't *know*," Mulhausser said, his voice getting thick again.

"All right, take it easy. What's her message?"

"My answering machine only records one minute on each call," he told me, exerting control. "Odile called twice in succession. I've recorded them on a regular cassette player so you can hear it all without the interruption."

"I'm listening." I heard the click of the player being switched on, very close to the phone. And then I heard her voice for the first time. A very young voice, halting and with an occasional tremor in it.

"Papa—this is Odile calling. I have to go away and I don't know for how long. Maybe I won't ever be able to see you again. If I don't . . . I just want to be sure you know . . . it *won't* be because I hate you. I don't—that was long ago."

There was a second's pause, as if she were searching for the right way to say what she wanted to. "I was a stupid kid. Now I'm older, I know how things can go wrong in a person's life. I *know* it's not your fault Mama was killed. If I acted badly when you drove me to Paris that night—it wasn't because I still blame you for that. . . ."

Again a slight pause, this time because the answering machine had cut her off and she'd had to make the second call. When she came on again her voice was very small. And she *was* crying.

"I was just very *ashamed* that night. When I needed someone and realized *you* were the only one there I could depend on to help me. There are only two people in the whole world I can count on completely . . . and you're one of them. And that made me think about how horrible I've been to you for so long.

"Goodbye, Papa. . . . If we don't ever see each other again, please forgive me. I'm so sorry. . . . I was such a rotten daughter . . ."

There was the sound of her hanging up the phone.

When I spoke to Mulhausser again there seemed to be something wrong with my own voice. "I'll *find* her," I told him.

I carried my bag out to the Peugeot and headed for Florence.

⊠ 26 ⊠

YOU'D HAVE TO GET VERY UNLUCKY TO HAVE YOUR CAR searched crossing the frontier from France into Italy. Especially if you show a U. S. Passport. Unless the control posts have a specific alert on you or have orders to do large scale spot-checks. And it's easy to detect the latter ahead of time by the massive blockage of angry motorists.

So the gun I'd stashed back in its secret rear-seat compartment didn't worry me much. Even so, I didn't try to cross via the high-speed autoroute. There are too many border guards assigned to that major crossing point. They can take turns, half of them playing cards inside their control buildings while the other half amuse themselves stopping cars to give their sense of authority a little exercise.

Instead I went through the end of Menton by way of Boulevard Garavan, a winding two-lane road that brings you to the oldest and smallest control point, halfway up the slope between the sea and the autoroute. It's the Pont St. Louis, a short bridge spanning a deep ravine that forms a natural separation between the two countries.

The two guards on the French side were having a conversation inside their little building, and they waved me on without bothering to come out. On the Italian side of the bridge I held up my passport and the guard motioned for me to keep going. Americans heading into Italy with their money are given every encouragement to move on to where they can spend it without delay.

As soon as I got to Ventimiglia, the first town in Italy, I did cut up onto the autoroute. On that side of the border they call it an autostrada, but it's a continuation of the same: a multilane toll expressway built to carry you over long stretches with a maximum of speed and a minimum of scenery. South of the border half the autostrada runs through a series of long tunnels. Arlette Alfani once kept count: 168 of them. In and out of the tunnels, I reached Florence in just over four hours.

It was a little after eight, with a low sun casting a reddish-golden glow over the square towers and Tuscan rooftops of what has to be one of the two or three loveliest Renaissance cities of Europe. Gilbert Lucca had booked his room at a pensione called the Villa Romana. It was on the Via dei Neri, behind the Uffizi. He hadn't arrived there yet.

The pensione's proprietor, Enio Pasqua, was a lanky man with sandy hair and an elegant nose. With the Florentine economy so dependent on foreign visitors, a pensione owner has to speak a couple of extra languages. Pasqua's were German and English, which was a help because my Italian was not that good. He told me Gilbert Lucca had phoned an hour ago to say he wouldn't get there until late that night, around eleven. He didn't know where the call had been made from.

Like the army, detective work involves a lot of "hurry up and wait." Popping in a couple of paperback books when I packed for a trip had long ago become automatic. It was the best way to pass the stretches of waiting. I'd gotten most of my education that way, while working. You don't get to read much in college—you're too busy figuring out exactly how your professors want their exam questions answered.

I stuck the book I'd brought along in my jacket pocket and went to dinner.

Florence is a small city, and its central streets were constructed long before automobiles were invented, making it a much easier place to walk than to drive. I walked to the Ponte Vecchio, the five-hundred-year-old, shop-lined pedestrian bridge. A triumph of respect for aging beauty over the demands of expediency. The only bridge across the Arno that the retreating German army didn't have the heart to destroy in order to slow the Allied troops in World War

II. They blocked access to it instead, by blowing up the houses at both ends.

I crossed the river and walked to Giovanni's, across from the fifteenth-century church of Santo Spirito. Most of the good Florentine restaurants that don't dip into your wallet too deeply are on that side of the Arno. I found Giovanni's steaks as thick and juicy as I'd remembered them.

Afterwards I strolled back across the Arno to a pleasant bar on the Piazza della Signoria. I passed the rest of my evening's enforced wait at a window table with a brandy and my book.

The one I was reading at the time was Gregory of Tours's *History of the Franks*. I was up to the year 590. With Queen Fredegund, who had recently attempted to strangle her daughter, having three noblemen chopped to mince-meat with axes at her banquet table. While her country's common folk were struggling to survive one of their harshest years of famine and floods, earthquakes and roving mercenaries, arctic winter and bubonic plague.

In a way it was comforting reading. A reminder that people's lives nowadays were no more trouble-prone than they'd ever been.

But in venerable Florence I didn't need the book for that. All I had to do was look out the bar's window. At the piazza where Savonarola burned Botticelli paintings his Christian purity crusade considered indecent; and where he himself was later burned to death for being an infernal nuisance. Or across at the Palazzo Vecchio, where people who'd plotted to assassinate Lorenzo the Magnificent were tossed out the tower windows with hangman's nooses around their necks.

None of which did much to relieve the pressure of my having to just sit there and wait while Mulhausser's daughter was in desperate trouble and I still hadn't found her.

At eleven that night I returned to the Villa Romana—and found the pensione's proprieter scowling and shaking his head.

"Gilbert Lucca phoned ten minutes ago. His van broke

down. He and a friend are trying to fix it. He will stay with his friend tonight. *Now* he says he will come in the morning. By bus if the van can't be fixed by then. Because he has appointments with shops, and he—"

I interrupted him with as much restraint as I could manage. "Where was he calling from?"

The question puzzled Enio Pasqua. "I don't know."

"You didn't ask where his friend's place is?"

"No. That's not my concern. *My* concern is the room I held for him, when I could have rented it to someone else. Now it's too late for that. I lock the doors at midnight."

And I had another frustrating wait ahead.

I took Gilbert Lucca's room and slept.

Gilbert Lucca arrived at eight the next morning.

I was having the pensione's breakfast of coffee and buttered rolls, in the small dining alcove off the smaller lobby, when he came in. He was carrying a lot of weight: two black salesman's cases, hung from his strong shoulders by thick straps, and a canvas bag in one muscular, long-fingered hand. He set them down and told Enio Pasqua that he was Gilbert Lucca.

After that he was speaking in rapid Italian. I had to concentrate to get some of it. He was apologizing for the previous night. His van required further repairs. He'd finally had to leave it with is friend in Siena and had come to Florence by bus. He expected to stay for one night.

I interrupted him in French. "We'd better have a talk before you decide anything."

He turned and frowned at me, trying to decide if he knew me. "I'm sorry," he said politely, switching to French, "but I'm afraid I don't—"

"It's about Odile."

He went still for a couple seconds. Then he said something quiet to Pasqua and came into the dining alcove, walking toward me slowly and warily.

When he reached my table I said softly, "It's all right. I'm not from the police. And I'm not one of the other people she's afraid of. Her father sent me to help her."

He didn't sit down, and he didn't say anything. Just stood there considering what I'd said and studying my face. I studied his in turn. From the snapshots I'd thought of him as a boy. In person he looked older. Not in years, but in what he'd acquired from those years. He looked capable and self-contained, with resolute eyes and a firm, uncompromising mouth.

This was someone I would have to play carefully, or I wouldn't get anything at all out of him.

I said, "You're right not to trust me until I give you reason to." I pushed back my chair and stood up. "The main post office is a five-minute walk. We can put through a long-distance call to her father, and you can talk to him. Then *we'll* talk."

I started toward the little lobby, but Gilbert Lucca stayed where he was, still eyeing me suspiciously. I turned to face him. "She phoned her father yesterday morning," I said, "and left a message on his answering machine. She told him there are only two people in the world she can depend on, and he's one of them. I guess you're the other one she meant. But you don't understand how much danger she's in—or you wouldn't have left her alone."

That bothered him. I walked out through the lobby. This time he followed, pausing to ask Enio Pasqua to watch his bags. Outside he walked silently beside me. Not a word, all the way to the Piazza della Repubblica and into the post office. We went into the telephone section, and I let him have information check Egon Mulhausser's two numbers in Eze, so he'd know I wasn't tricking him. And I let him make the call.

He tried Mulhausser's home number first and got him there. He told him he was a friend of Odile's and wanted to be sure who I was. Then he handed me the phone.

"This is Sawyer," I told Mulhausser. "The young man you just talked to is the one in the snapshot I showed you. The one your wife liked the look of. I do, too, but he's suspicious, and that's sensible of him. Just assure him that I'm working for you and that he can trust me."

I gave Gilbert Lucca back the phone and walked to the

cashier's counter, waiting for him there. When he hung up I paid for the call, and we walked out together.

"I had to be sure of you," he said.

"You did the right thing. And now you can relax. Where is she?"

"Where she's safe," he told me. "I'm not going to let you go there and walk in on her without me. Odile would think I betrayed her."

I registered the stubbornness in his expression and put a clamp on my impatience. "Let's go have an espresso."

We crossed to the nearest of the three big cafés on the piazza and took an inside table in the rear, where we could talk without being overheard. What I'd said to him back at the *pensione* still bothered him. When the waiter went to get our espressos Gilbert spoke.

"You have to understand—I didn't *want* to leave Odile alone. But I had to come down here. I need to make some money, for both of us. Odile doesn't have any left. And my business has gotten very tight lately. You know what the French economy has been like. Most of my French customers don't want to buy any more until they sell off most of their present inventories. I barely managed to pay my rent last month."

"Odile *could* get help from her father," I said. "All she has to do is ask him."

"I know that. And Odile knows it, too. But . . ." Gilbert made a helpless gesture. "She's too embarrassed to go to him. She says she acted too viciously toward her father—for too long." He paused and then added, with an uneasy pride, "I'm the *only* one she'll let help her now."

He paused again, trying to sort out his dilemma and explain it to me. "So I had to come down here. To get us at least a little income right now—and set up sources for more in the near future. I have some good customers in this part of Italy." Gilbert shook his head, frowning. "But . . . Odile wouldn't come with me. She's afraid of moving around too much. Of having too many people see her."

"She's right."

"Maybe. So I had to leave her—but in a place where

she's safe until I get back. If my van hadn't broken down, I could have finished up here in Florence today and been back with her tonight. To make sure she's all right, before coming down again.''

The waiter brought our cups and went away.

I said, ''Your're not enough protection for her, Gilbert. You're intelligent enough to know that. You don't have any experience in dealing with the kind of trouble Odile is in. I do have that experience. There's no way *you* can get her out of this mess. I can. That's my business.''

He sat there for a long time, his face hard as conflicting needs and desires did battle inside him. I watched him. Neither of us touched our espressos.

Finally he said, ''I can't let you see Odile unless I'm there, too. I have to be there, so she feels safe. So she knows you can't force her do anything she doesn't want to. Look, my *camionnette* will be repaired by tomorrow afternoon. Then I'll *take* you to Odile. All right?''

''No,'' I told him flatly. ''You want to take me to her, fine. But you have to do it *now*. Odile's father will pay the repair costs on your van and your fare to come back and pick it up. All you'll lose is a day. Odile could be dead by tomorrow. Get that through your head. Some very rough people are after her.''

''They won't find her,'' he said with absolute assurance.

''Don't be a fool. Of course they'll find her. It's just a matter of time. Like I found *you*. And I don't have as many people working on it as they do. If *they* were the ones who'd found you today, you wouldn't be sitting here having a coffee with them. You'd be someplace where nobody could hear your screaming, so they could torture you until you gave them Odile. They're *that* kind of people.''

I watched his assurance waver. ''I know,'' he said softly.

''Do you also know what she stole from them?''

''No.'' But it was an uncertain negative. He had *some* idea. He asked me, ''Do *you*?''

I told him. ''Three million dollars worth of pure heroin.''

His eyes squeezed shut. When they snapped open they

were as scared as I wanted them to be. "That crazy little idiot—"

"You must have known."

"Not *that* much."

"My car's near the *pensione*," I said. "Are we going?"

He nodded slowly. "But I won't tell you where—until we get to Odile. I'm not giving you any chance to drop me along the way."

"We'll have a hard time getting close," I pointed out dryly, "unless you at least give me a general direction. North, west, south, or—"

"*I'll* drive," Gilbert told me.

We looked each other in the eye. Neither of us blinked. I finally nodded.

We drank our espressos, got our things from the *pensione*, and put them in my Peugeot. He drove us out of Florence and turned northeast on route A-11.

We were on our way back to France.

⊠ 27 ⊠

"THE FIRST TIME I SAW HER," GILBERT TOLD ME, "WAS in Villefranche. One Sunday when I had a stand at the flea market there. That was when I was seventeen. The year before my mother died and I moved to Paris. Odile stopped at my stand and started asking how much I was charging for some of the pieces of jewelry. We ended up haggling over the price of a brooch I'd made. And flirting a little at the same time. Just kidding around, you understand. She was only fifteen. But there was something about her . . ."

He smiled to himself. There was a very special tenderness in it.

"I finally sold her that brooch for less than it cost me to make. And she still has it."

He kept his eyes on the road while he spoke, driving fast and well. Not driving had its advantages: I was able to lean back and study him some more while I listened.

"Odile was staying in Villefranche with her aunt for a month that summer. The next three Sundays when I was there she came around to my stand, and we talked some more . . . flirted some more. Her aunt began sticking close, not saying anything, but you could see she was a little worried. Can't blame her. Odile was just a kid. But . . . sweet and funny. And with something a little sad, too, sometimes. That thing she had about her mother and father—though I didn't know about that until much later.

"Then her aunt took her back to Paris. And by the next summer I was up there, too. But I never tried to look her up. Tell the truth, I didn't even think about Odile again. I was too involved with trying to get my business started.

We didn't run into each other again until just over a year ago.''

He had begun talking after we'd passed the ancient town of Lucca, half an hour out of Florence. Once he started it kept coming out of him, as though he couldn't stop it. I got the feeling Gilbert had been needing to talk it out about Odile for some time—to someone with whom he didn't have to conceal any part of it.

"We were both coming out of one of those little cinemas on the Rue Champollion when we saw each other again."

I knew where he meant. A short, alleylike street near the Sorbonne and College de France, with six movie theaters in a row that showed very old films.

Gilbert said, "I like going there by myself now and then, for a couple hours of forgetting my own problems. Turned out Odile does, too. It was a Chaplin picture that night. *Limelight*. We came out at the same time. Odile recognized me first. Reminded me about Villefranche. And the brooch she'd bought from me . . .

"We ended up walking for miles that night. Up one side of the Seine, down the other. And I took her to another old film the next night. And after that—well, she wasn't a kid anymore. We fell in love. I never met anybody who could make me feel so full of life"—Gilbert's voice tightened a notch—"when she's in the right sort of mood."

"When did you realize she's an addict?" I asked him.

"Oh, I knew pretty soon." Gilbert's voice was steady, flat. But the pain came through. "I didn't want to believe it. But . . . I've got other friends who do hard drugs. I *knew*. The way Odile always wore long sleeves and would only make love in the dark. And those mood changes.

"Finally I told her I knew. That made us closer, in a way. Her not having to pretend any more and be afraid of how I was going to react whenever I did find out. It didn't change how I felt about her, though. Except to make me determined to break her out of the habit somehow."

Gilbert's face got a haunted look you don't see on many

twenty-one-year-olds—except after a particularly bad stretch of combat duty. ''Well, I *tried*. And she tried. She really tried to kick it. For my sake, mostly. It almost drove her crazy, though.''

''Does she shoot it in the vein, or just skin pops?''

Gilbert drew a shuddery breath. ''She mainlines.''

I'd known that would have to be the answer. Odile wouldn't have become desperate enough to snatch the shipment otherwise. ''How long has she been hooked?''

''Since before we met again. Almost two years now.''

''How did she go about trying to kick it?''

''Just staying off it—with aspirins and some downers. And me holding her when she started shaking. But—she could never hold out long enough.''

''Nobody can,'' I told him. ''Not without medical help.''

''I thought,'' Gilbert said, ''that maybe if we got her away from Paris for awhile . . . to someplace calm. I was able to get the use of an isolated cabin, in the hills above Menton. In February. We moved in there for a week, hoping that might do it.''

I shook my head. ''No way. I know too many addicts. And only *one* who ever made it cold turkey. A man who happens to have a kind of craziness that got him through it and out the other end. Nobody normal can handle that kind of agony. Except in a clinic where they pump enough substitute dope into you so you're not quite there through most of it. Like going through a very long operation.''

''We *tried* that,'' Gilbert told me darkly. ''One of the free clinics that specialize in that sort of cure. But Odile wouldn't stay there long enough. The substitutes they gave her did ease the pain. But she missed the high too much. Her nerves kept demanding that rush.''

There was only one way that would work for Mulhausser's daughter, I knew. She'd have to be committed to a private sanitorium she couldn't leave when she wanted to. And kept there until her ordeal was over. Whether she fell back into her addiction after the cure only Odile could control. Perhaps with Gilbert's help.

But there was no point in discussing that with him now. The first order of business was her immediate survival. And one thing I needed for that was as much information about what had happened as Gilbert could give me. I continued to let him get to it in his own way.

"The last time we tried . . . that was back in early April. Neither of us had enough money left at that point to buy her the shit anyway. So—one last big try to kick it. The hard way. I stayed with her every minute."

Gilbert's face clouded as he remembered that time. I saw his hands tighten on the steering wheel. "But she couldn't hold out. And finally she kissed me good-bye and cried . . . and went off to the South. To see if she could get more of the shit from the bastard who turned her on to it in the first place."

"Who?" I asked him quietly.

"All I know is his name is Tony something. Odile would never talk about him much. But she did tell me he gave it to her free—at first."

"That's standard," I told him. "Hook them young. Then you've got a lifetime customer."

"Young . . ." Gilbert repeated the word bitterly. "I'd *kill* this Tony if I ever met him. Odile was only *seventeen* when he gave her her first fix. And he kept giving them to her—until she couldn't get by without it."

His voice went harsh with anger. "And *then*—after she couldn't do without the stuff—he began making her work like a call girl for him. Only not for money, like with a regular call girl. To amuse some of his friends. This Tony would make her go to them . . . and do whatever they wanted. And he'd pay her for it with a little heroin each time."

"Was this around Cannes?" I asked him.

"There—and in Paris, too." His voice was shaky. I let him take time to regain control of himself.

My Peugeot was running low on fuel by then. We pulled into the next gas station on the autostrada. After filling up we had some lunch in the fast food shack next to the station. Then we were speeding north again—and Gilbert told me the rest of it.

"Odile stopped giving herself to Tony's friends after she met me again in Paris." Gilbert had himself and his voice back under tight control. "But it was hard. She *needed* her fix—and she had to pay for it. And before long we were both running out of money. Things got tight for me. And Odile—she sold some property she had in the country that she'd gotten from her aunt. And she drained her bank account dry—and all of that money went incredibly fast."

"It's expensive stuff. And you need more and more."

"I *know*," Gilbert growled. He repeated it more softly: "I know . . ." He took several breaths before continuing. "So she went off to see this Tony character again. In the south. And she said good-bye to me. Because she *knew* . . . and I knew . . . there was only one way she could get him to supply her with what she needed."

"But Tony fooled her," I said. "He turned her over to somebody else instead. A thug named Bruno Ravic."

Gilbert glanced at me, surprised. Then he looked back to the road ahead, his eyes narrowed. "Is that his name? Odile didn't tell me that."

"What *did* she tell you?"

"This thug Tony gave Odile to . . . he'd give her a fix. But making her beg for it, or pay for it, any way he wanted." Gilbert's voice had gotten a sick sound. "He . . . he was turning her into an *animal*."

His misery became too strong for him to continue for several moments. I said, "And one night Bruno had a lot of heroin in his place. Just turned over to him, for delivery to Paris. And Odile snatched it after he fell asleep."

Gilbert nodded. "She told me that. She *didn't* tell me how *much* she took. I thought maybe enough for a month or so . . ."

"She took enough to last the rest of her life," I told him. "So she'd never have to buy any more—or do anything else to get it."

"She came back to Paris," Gilbert went on after a moment. "Back to me—but only for one night. She told me she'd stolen some dope. From some rough people. And she didn't want me involved. I wanted her to stay with me. So I could protect her. But she said her only chance was to disappear—alone. And I couldn't force her to stay with me."

"So she borrowed a friend's apartment."

Gilbert glanced at me again. "You know about that, too." It worried him, but he tried to mask it.

"I was hired to find Odile," I said. "The trail led there."

"It belongs to a woman we both know. She was going to be away for a week. Enough time, Odile said, for her to think where to go next. She made me promise not to visit her there. To give her time to think. But I called her regularly, to make sure she was all right. And she promised to let me know before going anywhere else, whatever she decided."

"And she finally decided to come south with you," I said, keeping my tone casual.

"Yes. . . . You see, the biggest Paris shop I sold to suddenly went out of business—owing me a lot of money I'd been depending on getting. So I decided I had to come south, try to stir up new business along the Côte d'Azur, and make some fast sales to my regulars in Italy. I called Odile and asked her to go with me. She finally agreed."

I could see him making an effort to keep his own tone casual—and to think carefully as he spoke. I asked, "When did you pick her up from that apartment?"

"Late Thursday night. She had all her things ready when I got there. We put them in my van, and I drove the rest of the night. I got to Menton in the morning."

"There was a man in that apartment," I said. "Medium height, sharp face. He had a gun with a silencer on it. His name was Maurice Bolec, and he worked for Tony. Which one of you killed him?"

I shouldn't have asked it at that moment. The Peugeot was doing 130 kilometers an hour, and Gilbert had it in the far left lane to pass slower cars. I saw his spasm of shock, and the car swerved for one horrible instant. It came within an inch of crashing into the concrete barrier that divided our northbound traffic from the southbound lanes.

He straightened the Peugeot in the last possible second and slowed down abruptly, still in shock. The horn of a car directly behind us blared wildly as the panicked driver applied his brakes to keep from ramming us.

"Speed up," I snapped at Gilbert.

He did so automatically.

I looked back. "You're clear on the right. Start swinging over toward the shoulder—without slowing down."

Again he obeyed like a robot. When he reached the far right lane he followed my next instruction, pulling off the autostrada and stopping the car on the paved emergency shoulder. He set the hand brake, cut the ignition, and turned to look at me with terrified eyes.

"He's *dead*?"

There was no doubt about it, Gilbert's surprise and fear were genuine.

"Very." I told him how I'd found Maurice over twenty-four hours after Gilbert and Odile had left the apartment.

Gilbert was beginning to come out of the shock. I watched him start to think coherently again. Finally he said, "I didn't *mean* to hit him that hard. I didn't know I *had* . . . hard enough to kill him. We thought he was just *unconscious*."

I believed his last sentence.

"Whatever was intended," I asked, "it was you who hit him with that candlestick?"

"Yes. I told you that."

I kept any disbelief out of my voice. "Nobody's going to cry over the death of a thug like Maurice. He was a professional killer, and he liked the work. He wanted to kill me not so long ago. And I know you must have done it in self-defense, or to protect Odile. How did it happen?''

He answered, slowly: "When I went to pick up Odile there, that night . . . I got there and heard her scream something inside . . . and I heard this man's voice, threatening her. The door was locked. I banged on it and yelled for them to let me in. . . .''

Gilbert paused to think about what he was going to say next, I let him take the time.

"This man opened the door and let me in," he resumed. "*Ordered* me to come in. He had that gun, and he made me stand beside Odile. She was terrified. He was saying what his friends would do to her, if she didn't tell him where to find what she'd taken from them."

That confirmed what I'd suspected about Maurice's reason for coming after Odile alone. He'd wanted to be the one who found that heroin. What he'd have done after he got it was a question I couldn't answer, because the answer had died with him. Maybe he'd intended to cover himself with glory by single-handedly showing up with Odile and the dope. Or maybe he would have killed her, hidden it, and later tried to peddle it himself.

"I knew," Gilbert went on, "that once they took Odile away I would never see her again alive. So I jumped him, grabbing his gun hand so he couldn't shoot me. We struggled and fell against the fireplace. I picked up that candlestick and hit him with it. He fell down, and . . . we thought he was only unconscious. And we were scared his friends might show up any minute. We grabbed Odile's things and got out of there as fast as we could. We *didn't* know he was dead. Anyway, it *was* self-defense."

"Yes," I agreed, "it was."

It hadn't happened the way he told it, though. I believed the last part: that they'd fled in panic, thinking Maurice was only knocked out and would come to later. But there was no way Gilbert could have jumped a pro like Maurice when they were standing face to face without getting shot before he could reach him.

The earlier part of what Gilbert had told me fitted what

I'd found there. His hearing Maurice and Odile inside the apartment. And banging on the locked door and yelling. That would have startled Maurice, twisting him toward the door.

Which had put Odile behind Maurice—just long enough for *her* to grab that candlestick and club him with it. His finger had squeezed the trigger as he fell and died, firing the bullet into the door frame.

"Oh my God"—Gilbert suddenly whispered in horror as a thought struck him—"I didn't wipe the *fingerprints* off that candlestick! It didn't occur to me. But if he's *dead*—"

"It's all right," I told him gently. "*I* wiped her prints off it."

He stared at me, not denying now that Odile had done it.

I told him, also, what I'd done about Maurice's body—so the cops would shrug it off as a gangland kill.

He went on staring at me—relieved, but puzzled. "You took a chance like that . . . *Why*?"

"Her father hired me to help her," I said. "I told you, that's my business."

We crossed the frontier and reentered France without incident. Gilbert turned sharply north onto Route 566, a mountain road that twists up into the Maritime Alps above Menton.

I said, "This safe place where Odile is holed up—"

Gilbert interrupted tightly, "I'm *still* not going to tell you where it is until we get there."

"I just hope it's not a hotel room."

"Of course not. It's a cabin in the mountains up there."

I had a bad feeling. "The same cabin you used when you came down with her from Paris in February?"

"It's exactly what we needed—that time and now. A place off by itself. Nobody else anywhere around it."

"How did you come by this cabin?"

"It belongs to one of my customers. He owns a boutique

in Paris, and he has this cabin for summer holidays. He let me have the key to it.''

I thought about all of Gilbert's business records—the ones the opposition had lifted from his place a few days ago.

My bad feeling got worse.

⊠ 28 ⊠

THE VAL DES MERVEILLES SPRAWLS ACROSS A VAST AREA at an altitude of seven thousand feet, encircled by blocky, barren crags rising two thousand feet higher. A rugged and almost entirely uninhabited region some thirty miles inland from Menton. As soon as Gilbert turned into the left-hand road after the hamlet of St. Dalmas, just above the Roya gorges, I knew that was where we were going.

That road doesn't lead anyplace else. And like the few other approach roads to the high valley, it ends before penetrating the heart of it.

I knew the area. My mother had taken me on a three-day camping trek through it when I was thirteen. Babette had wanted a firsthand look at the mysterious prehistoric symbols chiseled on the cliffs there. And I'd made a couple of trips since, with friends who'd wanted to see them.

No evidence has been found that any people ever lived in that area. Yet there are those symbols—almost forty thousand of them, by archeologists' count—made by unknown hands long before recorded history, for purposes no one has been able to fathom. Therefore the name it now bears: the Valley of Marvels.

The road we took toward it climbed steadily through steep, forested slopes via one sharp bend after another. We were above one side of a turbulent mountain stream that battered its way noisily down through a succession of fallen boulders. There were a few houses close together after St. Dalmas, then cabins spaced further and further apart; and then none for a couple miles.

We came to a cluster of fairly new alpine-style buildings beside a lake. It was a base for people to stay at when they came up into that area to hike or fish or investigate the prehistoric mysteries. But only one of the buildings was open now: a small café. Most visitors came to Val des Merveilles during the warm months of July and August. Now it was cold up there, in spite of a strong May sun beating down from a cloudless sky.

After passing the buildings we stopped the car to get warmer clothes from our bags. Gilbert had a sheepskin jacket. All I had was a wool turtleneck pullover. He watched thoughtfully when I took off the gun in its shoulder rig so I could pull on the sweater and then strapped it back in place before putting my jacket on over it. Then we drove on, always climbing.

The paved road ended, and we were on a gravel track. The trees around us thinned out, giving way to brush. There was an occasional cabin off to one side of the track or the other, each out of sight of the others. Above, the black rock formations of the Val des Merveilles came into view, almost denuded of vegetation. A region whose austere features bore evocative names: Devil's Peak, Black Lake, Malediction Pass.

I told Gilbert, "This is a hell of a place for her to be stuck in till you get back."

"It's not much further," he said, "and she's not *stuck* there. I rented her a little motorbike in St. Dalmas. She can get down there on it any time, in half an hour."

That was true. But the empty silence of this terrain made St. Dalmas seem much further away than that. The gravel track gave way to a wide path full of deep ruts and potholes—and stretches of mud where rivulets ran down from high springs. The Peugeot ground its way along through that for another mile. Then Gilbert pointed. "There it is."

A cabin squatted at the top of a narrow path that climbed around dark boulders off to our left. It had thick stone walls, a steep corrugated metal roof, heavy wooden shutters. There was smoke rising from its chimney and a motorbike leaning against the wall beside the closed door. I felt a surge of relief: there was no car but my own anywhere in sight.

Gilbert stopped the Peugeot at the bottom of the narrow

path to the cabin. There was no way to get it any closer. As we got out Gilbert said, "Please let me go first. I want to prepare her before she sees you. So she won't get scared."

I nodded. "But make it fast. Every hour we stick around gets more dangerous."

He hurried up toward the cabin, climbing the path with long strides. He knew the urgency now. I'd explained about the opposition taking his business records. The man who owned this cabin was prominently listed among them.

Gilbert was almost to the cabin when Odile came out of it. She was wearing a lumber jacket, corduroy trousers, and short hiking boots. I watched the way she ran to meet him, laughing as she threw her arms around him.

They were still holding each other when she saw me down beside the car. Her head jerked back as though she'd been slapped. The joy washed out of her face in a spasm of shock and terror. She tried to twist away from Gilbert. He seized her arms and began talking to her, swiftly and firmly.

When she stopped fighting him I began climbing the path, taking my time. Gilbert continued to speak to her, gradually relaxing his hold. She didn't run. He turned to face me with her, taking her hand in his.

By the time I reached them most of her fear had drained away. She stood beside Gilbert, staring at me with a mixture of confusion and hope. But the hope was obviously something she didn't believe in much.

It was my first slow, close look at Egon Mulhausser's daughter. I could see what Gilbert had fallen for. She had the look of a besmirched fairy princess, her eyes haunted, with dark smudges under them. But all the more touching for that—fragile and hurt, in need of someone to rescue and protect her.

"My . . . my *father* sent you . . ." she said in wonder.

"He's the one," I assured her. "We can talk it all out later. Right now we've got to get away from here. Before Tony Callega's associates show up."

Quickly Gilbert explained to her about their stealing his business records—and that, with those to work from, they were sure to get to the cabin's owner sooner or later.

I saw panic rise in Odile's eyes again—and I deliberately stoked it. "Not *later*. By now they *know* about this place. And they know you two used it before, in February. They're on their way while we stand here talking. So if you've got stuff to pack, do it fast."

I did want her to get ready quickly. But I wanted more than that. I wanted her to grab what was most precious to her. But it didn't work.

She stood where she was for several moments, thinking hard. And she looked up at the dark, looming formations of the Val des Merveilles. Then she nodded—to herself as much as to us—and walked back inside the cabin.

I went in close behind her, with Gilbert following. It was a snug room, warmed by a couple of small logs burning in the brick fireplace. A large bed and an old leather wing chair, a bureau and a rustic table with a couple of kitchen chairs. A standing closet next to a tiny kitchenette that took up one corner. A door to a small bathroom.

A canvas suitcase was open on the table, with some of Odile's things in it. She hadn't completely unpacked. I watched her snatch a worn leather shoulder bag off the bed and go into the bathroom with it, shutting the door behind her. I had a look inside her open suitcase while Gilbert doused the fire.

She came out quickly, dumped her shoulder bag on the bed again, and began tossing the rest of her clothes into the suitcase. Closing it, she picked up her shoulder bag again. "All right, I'm ready."

The shoulder bag was big enough to hold perhaps a couple of week's supply of heroin and additives for diluting it. Plus the usual addict's accessories: hypodermic needle, syringe, matches, makeshift cooker, tourniquet—the works. The rest of that heroin she'd hijacked was definitely not in the suitcase. She had out-thought me—with all the quick cunning of the desperate.

The way she figured it, in a couple of weeks it would

be safe for her to slip back here to pick up the rest. She had enough to last her until then. And by then the men after her would have come and gone.

She wasn't afraid of them finding that big load of heroin. So it wasn't in the cabin or close to it. I thought about the way she'd looked up at the black, disordered expanse of the Val des Merveilles—but that was too many miles to search.

"Where is it?" I asked her quietly.

Odile met my stare without flinching, her face gone tight and fierce—and suddenly not pretty at all. That was the other facet of her showing itself: the part created by the drug and the insatiable craving.

I asked Gilbert, "Was she carrying anything else when you brought her here? Besides that suitcase and shoulder bag. A knapsack—or anything else that size."

He knew what I was talking about. He said, "Odile . . . please." His voice was tormented by his helplessness in the face of a power that held her more strongly than their love.

She looked at him. Not the hard, ungiving look she'd turned on me. But still she wouldn't speak. She only gave him a single negative shake of her head. With absolute finality to it. His strong shoulders slumped, and he turned away.

"Odile," I said, "listen to me carefully. Really *listen*. They won't stop hunting for you as long as you have that stuff. Ever. You have to let me get rid of it—in a way that'll make them *know* you don't have it any more."

"They'll still kill me when they find me. For stealing it."

"I think I can handle that," I told her. "But not if they think you still have their merchandise. Do you understand that?"

"I understand one thing"—her voice had gone ragged—"if I give it away, how will I ever get more? And if I can't get more, what will I *do*?"

I knew the answer to that. It lay in locking her away in a place I knew where they had a fair record of curing addiction. She was legally an adult now, which meant it would be illegal to put her in there against her will. But it could be done if her father was willing to ignore the illegality—and take the chance that his daughter would go back to hating him for doing it.

But this was not the time to tell her I had that in mind for her. The first order of business *was* to get her away from there. And to stash her where I knew she'd be safe—and couldn't escape me. Once I had her there—and got rid of Gilbert—I could apply the kind of pressure that would make her tell where she'd hidden that big cache of heroin. Three days of not letting her have her fix should do it. It was going to be brutal—but there was no other way.

"You win," I told her. "Let's go."

I watched the brief flicker of triumph in her haunted eyes—and the way it was almost immediately drowned in a deep, knowing sorrow.

Gilbert followed me out of the cabin, carrying her suitcase. Odile came out after him. He was locking the cabin door when I heard it. I motioned for them to be quiet and I listened, looking toward the source of the sound, back along the rutted path Gilbert and I had used with the Peugeot.

It emerged around a tight bend. A Jeep. The right kind of vehicle for this region. Narrowing my eyes to slits, I could make out four men in it. Two in front, two in back.

We could reach my car before the jeep did. But there was no way to escape with the car. We couldn't go back the way we'd come. The jeep was there. In the other direction the path we'd driven led nowhere. And in this terrain the Peugeot had no chance of outdistancing a jeep.

"Drop the suitcase," I snapped at Gilbert, and I pointed toward the dark heights of the Val des Merveilles. "They can't follow us up there with that jeep. On foot we've got a chance."

Gilbert said shakily, "Maybe they're not after Odile. They could be just looking around the area, or—"

"We'll know that if they don't come after us," I snapped. "Move it!"

He threw aside the suitcase, grabbed Odile's arm, and started up the steep slope with her. I didn't tell her to throw away the shoulder bag. She would sooner have left her arm behind. I went up after them. They were young and strong, already climbing swiftly. I looked back.

The jeep had stopped behind my car. The four men were climbing out and starting up the slope after us.

One point in our favor: None of them carried a rifle. With a good rifle they could have dropped us from where they were. A hand gun wasn't any use at that distance. If we could stay ahead of them until dark, we could lose them.

One problem: There were hours left before night. Another problem: There was very little concealment up there where we were heading—few trees and only very low brush.

The third problem was that I didn't know how long it had been since Odile had had her last fix. If the need came to her before dark, she was going to start caving in on us. And a halt to let her shoot up would bring those four men on top of us.

I looked back again without slowing my pace. They were still the same distance behind us, no further, no nearer.

One of them looked like Tony Callega, though I couldn't be sure at that distance. Two of the others I didn't know at all.

Sheer size made the fourth man Boyan Traikov.

⊠ 29 ⊠

I LENGTHENED MY STRIDE AND MOVED UP AHEAD OF GIL-
bert and Odile, leading them toward an area I remembered.
There was too much danger in traveling any distance
through terrain I didn't know. In that vast jumble of hap-
hazard formations we could find ourselves trapped in the
end of a blocked gorge with no way to go but back—toward
the guns of our four pursuers.

Once into a section I was familiar with, we would have
an advantage. The four behind us were unlikely to know
the Val des Merveilles. They were reduced to trailing us
with no foreknowledge of what lay ahead—unable to detour
in order to get ahead of us. I wasn't going anywhere, just
aiming to keep away from them until dark.

Less than fifteen minutes from the cabin we slipped
through a break in a high ridge. Ahead of us was a section
I'd been through twice in the past. First with Babette. The
second time with three friends from Paris I took on a trek
to some of the paleolithic cliff engravings.

What lay below the other side of the ridge was a cirque
that spread for several miles. A steep-sided hollow gouged
into the land by long-vanished glaciers and bottomed by a
long, deep, meandering lake. The inner slopes above the
lake were precipitous, in places forming near-vertical cliffs.
Wherever soil had gathered in dips and fissures there were
patches of scrub with vividly colored alpine flowers. Here
and there a lone stunted pine had anchored itself into a split
in the rocks. But most of the cirque was dominated by
stone and water, both tinted a dark, shiny purple by the
sunlight.

I led the way down the steep inner face of the hollow,
warning Gilbert and Odile to place each footstep with care.

The slope there was littered with loose stones and erosion-splintered rock. A wrong move could start them rolling and sliding. There was little vegetation at this height to hold the land in place. Large expanses of exposed rock had been disintegrated by ages of weathering. That made many of the steeper slopes extremely unstable, with any minor slippage of debris liable to trigger a major landslide.

Odile seemed somewhat more surefooted then Gilbert as we made the descent.

I got the distinct impression she'd been this way before, without him.

We reached a ledge that ran along the slopes roughly fifteen feet above the edge of the lake. As we moved on along the ledge I looked back again. Boyan Traikov and the other three were making their way down from the break in the ridge to our ledge path. I was certain now: One of the others was Tony Callega.

I continued along the ledge with Gilbert and Odile, keeping to the same steady pace. Below us there were places where spurs of rock at the bottom of the slope jutted out just over the surface of the lake. At other points the dark water lapped over little beaches of pebbles and fallen, shattered boulders.

Our route took us around a number of sharp bends where for minutes at a time were were out of our pursuers' view. But at none of these places was there any other way through the cirque or out of it. Nothing we could do but stick with the ledge route. And Traikov and his men could see we had nowhere else to go, even when they couldn't see us.

That situation would change, I remembered, when we reached the other end of the lake. Once we climbed out of the cirque there, we would be into a maze of tight little gorges, each with a choice of several side-ravines and cross-gullies. *There* we could lose the pursuit, even in daylight.

It was just a matter of not letting the four men back along our trail get any closer before we got there.

For the first hour we had no difficulty keeping well ahead of Traikov's group.

Then Odile began to falter. Gilbert had to seize her arm and pull her along with him in order to maintain our pace. But she kept getting heavier and weaker, her feet dragging. I dropped back and took her other arm, helping Gilbert to hurry her along.

What was happening was obvious. Her face was drawn with strain and unnaturally pale. She was breathing harshly with her mouth open, her lungs heaving painfully. Prolonged drug abuse saps the user's natural health and strength. A fix injects a spurt of substitute energy into the veins—for a short time. But as that drains away the system goes into a collapse.

We were almost to the far end of the lake. But Odile was becoming a dragging weight between Gilbert and me, slowing us more and more.

"I've got to stop," she sobbed. She was trembling now. "Just a minute—please!"

I knew what she needed it for, and I knew it would take more minutes than we could survive. All the involved preliminaries. Getting a little water and preparing the syringe. Measuring the precise mixture. Heating the cooker. Tying the tourniquet on to pump out the vein. Traikov and company would have us before she could plunge the needle in.

But at the pace she was forcing us to, they were going to catch up with us anyhow—before we could climb out of this end of the cirque.

"Move her faster," I snarled at Gilbert. There was no time for explanations. Just ahead of us were two sharp bends in the slope, one immediately after the other. We almost carried Odile. Both bends created temporary screens between us and the pursuers.

I stopped immediately after we were around the second one, letting go of Odile. She sagged in Gilbert's arms, panting. I pointed at a wide rock spur just below our ledge: "It overhangs a small cave. Get out of sight under there, fast. I'll try to make them think you're still with me—draw them after me. If they fall for it, wait until they're well past you. Then get her back to the car—and down to Menton. Wait for me at the Piccadilly."

I left them and ran the rest of the way along the ridge. The pursuit group still hadn't appeared. I scrambled up a funnel in the scarp above that end of the lake. There were other ways I could have gone up, but this route was full of loose debris, and that was what I wanted.

I kept kicking the rubble as I made the climb, starting it rolling. By the time I neared the crest everything loose in the funnel was in motion below me. A little landslide, rumbling loudly down the slope, churning up dark clouds of rock dust that billowed high in the air.

I went over the crest in a low crouch and flopped down behind an eroded projection of stone. Flat down on my belly, I turned myself and eased forward to peer back down around the base of the projection.

Gilbert and Odile were gone from the ledge, out of sight under the overhang. One heartbeat later Boyan Traikov, Tony Callega, and the other two men appeared on the ledge, coming around the last bend. They halted, just above the point where Gilbert and Odile were hidden. But they didn't look down. They were looking up in my direction, where the clouds of slide still billowed and the last loose stones were dribbling down the funnel.

Then they were in motion again, quickly leaving the ledge behind and climbing toward my hiding place. They spread out as they came up the slope: Traikov and Tony Callega off to one side of the funnel, the other two on the other side.

I snaked backward. When I was far enough for the crest to screen me from the climbers I got my feet under me. Keeping low, I entered a shallow gully and went through to where it merged into a wide ravine. The ravine twisted between broken, jagged walls of mixed clay and stone. I went halfway through it and then hauled myself up one side.

A dead tree lay there, uprooted and smashed apart by a rock slide long ago. I lifted one end of its largest severed branch, got it balanced on the other end, and toppled it over the edge. It crashed to the bottom of the ravine. Not much dust this time. But enough noise to give my position

to the four men hunting me. I didn't want them to lose me.
Not yet.

The longer they kept trailing me, the more time Gilbert
and Odile would have to reach my Peugeot and get away.
I figured he would let her have her fix first. Under the
circumstances, that was the right thing to do. She wouldn't
make it all the way back to the car without that lift.

On my own I was going to have little difficulty staying
ahead of the pursuit force. I wouldn't even have to wait
for dark to make my escape. When I judged I'd given
Gilbert and Odile enough of a head start I would begin to
circle back. In this area—which I knew and the pursuers
didn't—I should be able to bypass them and make it to
their Jeep. With plenty of time to hot-wire its ignition before they returned. I'd use the Jeep—and they'd have a very
long walk.

It seemed a workable tactic—at the time.

I began climbing again, cutting between wind-hewn
spires of rock, following a route I knew. It took me, finally, to the mouth of a narrow gorge.

Near it was a small group of low, gnarled pine trees. I
made my way up to the trees and into their deep shadow.
Turning, I leaned against a bent trunk and looked back the
way I'd come.

Several minutes passed. Then I spotted two of the pursuers coming in my direction, shifting quickly and cautiously from the cover of one stone spire to the next.
Keeping about seven feet apart from each other. They were
good at this kind of stalking.

I stayed where I was, waiting. Looking for the other
two. The first pair emerged from the scattering of spires,
still well separated, and scanned the area where I was hidden. Each held a gun ready in one hand. These were the
two men I didn't know.

Concealed under the trees, I continued to search the area
behind them for Tony Callega and Boyan Traikov. They
didn't appear.

After a few moments the pair I could see started ad-

vancing toward my general area, spreading further apart.
They didn't glance behind them before doing so.

My heart sank.

One of them had gotten suspicious of how easy it was
for them to trail me by the noise I'd been making. Probably
Traikov—he was the brain of this bunch.

I'd underestimated that brain. His size and strength
tended to occupy all of one's attention. Reju had warned
me against that—back at the Cannes film festival. It seemed
a long time ago, and very far away.

This pair had continued to trail me. Tony and Boyan
Traikov had turned to recheck the back trail, just in case.

Back where I'd left Gilbert and Odile.

☒ **30** ☒

THERE WAS NO TIME LEFT FOR PLAYING HIDE-AND-SEEK with the pair of gunmen coming toward me now. I had to put them out of action fast and get back to Gilbert and Odile.

I drew my gun from its holster and fired a shot at one of them. Just to let them know where I was. At that distance I didn't have a chance of coming anywhere near the target with a pistol.

They instinctively dodged for cover but then stopped, looking at the point I'd fired from. Registering the distance and not even attempting to fire back. I went through the little pine grove and out the other side and then ran up an incline to the mouth of the gorge. As I entered it I looked back. The two gunmen were on the move again, coming after me—much faster now.

I headed up through the gorge. It was hard going, but I'd known it would be. The gorge climbed steeply, cutting up the side of a mountain. It was narrow, with sheer walls that rose some twenty feet on either side of me. In places it was partially blocked where slides had sent broken boulders and shale rolling down through the confines of the steeply inclined gorge.

The gunmen coming after me would be well inside the gorge by now. But they'd take their time working through each blockage, wary of ambush. I didn't have that to worry about. I went through as fast as I could.

I reached what I'd come in for. A place where the wall on my left stopped being sheer and became a climbable slope. Climbable—but dangerous.

Piles of rocks and thick slabs of shale covered all of the slope. Debris from higher slopes that had slid only partway

186

down. They formed an unstable mass of rubble. A land-slide waiting to happen.

But to one side of that loose mass was a relatively bare scar cutting upward through jagged formations. I worked my way up through the scar with infinite care. Even there, to one side, any stones I caused to roll could trigger the entire slope into movement.

I made it to the summit and turned to my left. There a top-heavy boulder perched precariously on the lip, its base eroded by runoffs from mountain rains. I waited there, looking down the length of the gorge below.

Minutes dragged by. Then I glimpsed movement among the rock rubble in the floor of the gorge. Hidden by the boulder, I continued to watch and wait. The two gunmen appeared, approaching cautiously, slipping from one bit of cover to the next, poised to shoot the instant they saw me. But they didn't see me—and they kept coming.

When they were almost directly below me I put my back to the boulder, spread my feet, and shoved with all my strength. The boulder leaned, tilted over the edge, and went crashing down the slope. As it rolled, the whole slope began to slide—slowly at first, and then very fast.

The two gunmen froze for an instant, staring up in horror at the tons of rock and shale thundering down at them. They tried to run. But there was nowhere for them to go in the brief time left to them. The downward-crashing slope had started the masses of rubble in the steep bottom of the gorge moving, too.

A dense, rising fog of rock dust shrouded their end. If they had time to scream before they were engulfed, it couldn't be heard through the noise of that ponderous land-slide.

I turned away and followed a route along the top of the gorge for a short time. Then I shifted to another route that took me down around a hogback, in the direction of the little grove of pines and the spires of stone. I pushed as fast as I could and ran where it was possible.

Back toward the cirque and its long, dark lake.

Gilbert wasn't far from where I'd left him with Odile. He was on the ledge that ran along the cliff wall above the water. He was crawling along it, back in the direction of the cabin. A long way to go, with one leg dragging uselessly.

I had my gun in hand when I reached him. But there was nobody else in sight.

Gilbert's right trouser leg had a bullet hole above the knee and was soaked with blood. He had knotted his belt around his upper thigh to staunch the bleeding. When I arrived he turned, wincing at the pain, and leaned against the cliff, resting on his left hip. His nose was bleeding, too. It had been broken.

He spoke through clenched teeth. "I let her go down to get water for her shot. Five minutes after they'd gone past. I thought it was safe then. But two of them came back . . . and saw her coming up to the cave. A very big man, and a smaller one . . . the one she calls Tony. He's the one smashed my nose with his gun."

"Did she shoot up before they grabbed you?" It was important to know what condition she was in.

Gilbert nodded. "Just before they came in at us. They said they'd kill me if Odile didn't tell them where the dope is. Then Tony shot me in the leg—and swore he'd come back and kill me if she was lying to them."

That was the only reason he was still alive. So Odile would take them to her heroin cache in order to save him. "*Where* did she tell them it is?"

"Back near the other end of the lake. Not far from the cabin." Gilbert nodded at the pistol in my fist. "You've got to hurry. They'll kill her once they have that dope."

"I'll come back for you," I told him, and I left him there, heading in the direction they'd taken.

I ran most of the way along the side of the lake. But when I was about two-thirds of the way to the end I slowed to a silent walk and worked at getting my breathing back under control. *They* hadn't been running. I had to be getting close to them by then.

I stopped at each bend in the cliff that hid the way ahead.

Stopped and listened—before easing around the bend, leading the way with the H&K, my finger ready on its trigger.

I was almost at the last bend before that end of the lake when I heard them—very close ahead.

Their voices stopped me. When I moved again it was without a sound. I still couldn't see them. But I could hear.

Boyan Traikov's matter-of-fact voice: "Behind this? You're quite sure?"

I didn't hear Odile. She either whispered or answered with a gesture.

Tony Callega's voice, edgy and exultant: "It better *be* there, Odile—or your boyfriend is *dead*."

I eased around the jut of rock. Tony stood with his back to me, a long-barreled revolver dangling in one hand, watching Traikov and Odile.

She sat on the lip of the ledge, her head bowed in hopeless defeat, her legs hanging over the water that sloshed under the rocks ten feet below.

Traikov was down on one knee beside her, gripping her wrist with one hand. His other hand had reached down below the ledge and pulled away a slab of stone, letting it fall into the lake with a loud splash. He was reaching into a hole there when I made my move.

I took a long stride and clubbed Tony Callega's skull with my gun, just behind the ear, very hard. He went down and out. His body made a half turn as he fell. He sprawled unconscious across the ledge, one leg straight and the other bent, the revolver falling from his limp hand.

Traikov was in motion before I could twist around to cover him with my gun. His move was sure and swift. It brought him to his feet with the knapsack hanging from one hand, his other hand yanking Odile upright between us to shield him from my gun. He dropped the knapsack on the ledge, and that hand shot up to grip Odile's neck.

I raised my gun to take aim at Traikov's head. He ducked, getting his head behind hers. At the same instant he shifted his grip on her. One hand caught hold of her chin, the other fastened on the back of her skull.

"One little twist," he said flatly, "and she's a dead girl."

Odile stared at me, frozen in the grasp of his huge hands.

I lowered my aim to the side of his left hip. "You're too big to hide all of you behind someone that small."

"Go ahead and shoot," he said. "And I snap her neck and toss her at you."

"Then you'll both be dead," I told him thinly.

"Not sure." From his tone we might have been discussing the best way to cut a cake. "Small caliber bullets like you've got there, the first shot won't hurt me much. You might even get in a second shot before I'm on top of you. But unless you get very lucky, I'll still kill you barehanded before you can take the third shot. Do we try it—or do you throw your gun away?"

I hesitated. Because he could be right, on every point.

"Your choice," Traikov said evenly. "You got three seconds. Then I break her neck, and we find out who dies next, you or me. I'm ready if you are."

I believed him. I threw the gun away, out over the lake. Traikov dropped his hands to grasp Odile's arms and automatically turned his head to watch it splash into the water. In that instant I launched myself at him and Odile, ramming them with a low driving tackle.

It caught him by surprise. He hadn't expected to have any problem with me once I was unarmed. And holding Odile made him a fraction too slow in spreading his feet to regain his balance.

The three of us toppled off the edge and fell to the deep water below.

⊠ **31** ⊠

I HOPED THREE THINGS IN THE SPLIT SECOND BEFORE WE hit the surface of the lake:

That Traikov couldn't swim as well as I could. That he hadn't filled his lungs with air in the last instant, like I had. And that he wasn't prepared for the freezing temperature of mountain water at that altitude.

It was like plunging deep down into solid ice.

Even though I was expecting it, I had to use all my willpower not to gasp at the shock of it, which would fill my lungs with water. And I had to keep my eyes open.

Traikov let go of Odile as we sank. I saw her drift away from us. Traikov, momentarily disoriented by the shock of the plunge, flailed his arms and legs in a wild attempt to get his head above water. I didn't let him.

Grabbing one of his arms with both hands, I spun him deeper with me and swung myself behind him. Continuing to drag him down, I locked my legs around his so he couldn't use them properly and seized two fistfuls of his hair. I yanked his head back sharply. The force of it snapped his mouth wide open. If he hadn't been breathing water before that, he did then.

His elbows struck back at me. It hurt, but not as much as it would have out in the air. Up there my ribs would have cracked under those blows. But the density of the water slowed and cushioned them.

Traikov stopped trying that—or anything else to break my grip on him. He became too occupied with trying to pull us both up to where he could breathe air. I fought against it, twisting us underneath a wide spur of partly submerged rock. And lowered my head just in time.

Traikov, increasingly disoriented, didn't see it. With his

next spasm of effort to reach the surface the top of his skull struck the underside of the projecting rock. The flailing of his arms became weaker and less coordinated. His head was clouding from the blow and from lack of oxygen. I shoved him further under the rock, using the push to drive myself away from him and out from under it.

My head broke the surface. I sucked in the air greedily, sending relief to my tortured lungs.

Odile had climbed out of the lake. She was scrambling back up to the ledge, water streaming from her hair and clothing. I stroked to the same point. My blood was racing, too heated by battle for me to feel how cold I was yet. But when I tried to get a grip on the shore rocks my hands fumbled. They were going numb.

The only cure for that was movement. I concentrated on closing my fingers around a couple of handholds, and I hauled myself out. I slapped my hands against my thighs. Wet against wet. My soaked clothes were pasted to my skin. The air was hitting me like more ice. No time to give that any attention. The priority was to get to Tony Callega's gun before he come to. And before Traikov, if he made it to the surface, came after me.

I began to climb after Odile. Then Traikov surfaced, noisily. I twisted around to check his distance from me. He wasn't far. But he was entirely occupied, for the moment, with staying afloat while he coughed out water and gasped in air.

A gunshot sounded behind me.

I turned, knowing the worst before I saw it.

Odile stood over Tony Callega's sprawled figure, holding his revolver in both hands. While I watched she fired a second time. I saw his head bounce on the ledge as the shot slammed into it.

Quickly, I looked back to Boyan Traikov. He was treading water, looking up toward Odile. Worse and worse.

I scrambled the rest of the way to the ledge. Odile hadn't moved. She was staring down at Tony Callega's body. Her face was empty of expression, and she was beginning to shake—not just from cold.

I held out my hand to her. "Let me have the gun, Odile."

She turned her head, looking at me without comprehension for a moment. Then her eyes focused. She put Tony's revolver in my hand and raced away, running back toward where they'd left Gilbert.

I turned and took dead aim at Boyan Traikov. He had shucked his waterlogged jacket. Probably kicked off his shoes, too. When he saw me train the gun on him he began swimming away as fast as he could. But he was still in easy range. I drew a bead on the back of his head.

And couldn't do it.

There was reason to. Traikov had seen Odile kill Tony. That was going to put her in worse danger than she'd been in before—if he lived to report it to Fulvio Callega.

But I couldn't make myself shoot an unarmed man who was floundering in the middle of a lake and posed no immediate threat to me.

The crazy bastard hadn't even been carrying a gun. He did carry men with him who had guns. But none of his own. Some quirky private brand of pride. Proof to himself, perhaps, that he'd risen above acting as somebody else's gun-toter. Crazy.

When seconds passed without my shooting, Boyan Traikov twisted to look back at me. If there was surprise in his expression, I couldn't make it out. I looked down the sights of the revolver at his face and shouted, "Keep going! The other side of the lake!"

Traikov continued to gaze at me for a long moment. Then he nodded and began to swim again—toward the other side of the lake.

He wasn't a bad swimmer, but he wasn't great, either. And he had a long way to go. Maybe he would drown before he could get there. Or freeze to death after he climbed out. I hoped so. But I doubted it.

I stuck the revolver in my belt and looked down at Tony Callega again. The first shot had gotten him in the chest. The second had smashed through his mouth and come out his ear. Not pretty. Chantal Jacquier wasn't going to have him for her bridegroom after all. Odile had accomplished that, at least. Whoever Chantal eventually married, he would have to be better for her than a Tony Callega.

I suddenly realized I was trembling with cold. I stripped off my wet jacket, sweater, and shirt. Tony's fleece-lined jacket and cashmere cardigan had his blood on them. At that point I didn't give a damn. I stripped them off him and put them on.

The cardigan was too small for me. I had to stretch it out of shape to get it buttoned. It was impossible to close and button his lined jacket, and the sleeves were too short. But the combination did give me some dry warmth.

Boyan Traikov was still swimming off in the direction I'd ordered, awkwardly but steadily. I jogged in place to stir my blood and body heat while I watched him go. When he was almost halfway across the lake I looked to where he'd dropped the knapsack with its load of heroin. It was still there. Not far from it Odile's shoulder bag lay on the ledge against the base of the cliff. I left them there and jogged off to get Odile and Gilbert.

I was still sore at myself for not having the guts to shoot Traikov. A failure that saddled me with an enormous new problem. While I ran I tried to work it out. What was I going to do about Tony Callega's big brother?

Odile was kneeling beside Gilbert, tightening the belt tourniquet around his thigh. He had put his sheepskin jacket on her small, trembling form and was buttoning it.

I crouched and pulled his right arm across my shoulders, then I straightened up until I had him standing, balanced on his good leg. Odile took the other side, with his left arm braced over her slim shoulders, grasping his wrist with both hands. Between us we helped him take that long, painful walk, one-legged, back toward the cabin.

It was heavy work, but the exertion worked against the cold. By the time we reached the place where Tony Callega lay we were sweating. We stopped, and I looked across the lake. Boyan Traikov was still afloat and swimming and almost at the other side.

Picking up the knapsack, I checked on whether it still held the heroin. It did: almost a full load. I gathered my wet jacket, sweater, and shirt, tied them to one strap of the knapsack, and hung it over my right shoulder.

I let Odile take her shoulder bag. She would need what was left in it to keep functioning until I got her where I wanted her.

Traikov crawled out of the other side of the lake. I watched him stand up, take a couple steps, and fall down. Maybe he was going to die after all. No such luck—not with a powerhouse like Traikov. He forced himself up and began a stumbling run along the lake shore. Just to fight his numbing cold; not with any expectation of reaching the two vehicles ahead of us. From that side of the lake it would take a couple hours to get around to there. We would be gone long before he could make it.

Odile and I got Gilbert up out of the cirque, and then down to the cabin. It was still blessedly warm inside. Odile brought in her suitcase. While she toweled herself dry and changed into other clothes I got my bag from the Peugeot. Then it was my turn with a dry towel and a change of clothing.

I stuffed my wet things in my bag. I put it back in my car, along with Tony's jacket and cardigan—to be thrown on the fire of a public dump halfway down to the coast.

Then we got Gilbert down to the Peugeot. I laid him on the back seat and put Odile up in front. After which I used the revolver's last three bullets to shoot out three of the Jeep's tires. Give Boyan Traikov a little more warm-up exercise.

I wiped the revolver clean of prints and buried it under some thornbushes. Then I tied the motorbike to the back of my car, to be given back in St. Dalmas, and drove us away from Val des Merveilles.

On the way I began giving more thought to what I was going to do about Fulvio Callega.

◙ 32 ◙

In St. Dalmas I phoned Egon Mulhausser. When we reached his house in Eze he was there waiting for us—together with Libby Arlen and a doctor I'd asked him to call.

When Odile got out of my car she and her father stood there looking at each other uncertainly, not speaking. It was obvious that Mulhausser wanted to take her in his arms, but he was afraid to make the first move. Odile made it for both of them, hugging him tightly. Her father awkwardly patted her back. She nestled her face against his shoulder—and then pulled away, suddenly embarrassed.

Mulhausser brushed a hand across his eerie, lashless eyes and then helped me get Gilbert into the house. Libby Arlen put her arm around Odile's waist, and they followed us inside, together with the doctor.

His name was Henri Pinel, and I'd known him a very long time. Long enough to ask a couple of favors. The first being that he treat Gilbert's leg as an accident caused by a fall onto a sharp stake—and not report it as a gun wound. We put Gilbert on the bed in the guest room. Dr. Pinel shooed us out so he could tend to Gilbert alone. I had a quiet word with Dr. Pinel before following the others. He gave me a frowning nod and shut the door behind me.

Odile was beginning to shiver again. I suggested she'd better take a long hot bath to ward off fever. Libby Arlen went upstairs with her to draw the bath and get some towels. As I'd expected, Odile took her shoulder bag up there with her.

I could have used a soak in a hot tub myself. But I settled for having Mulhausser get me a large glass of brandy. Odile

197

and Libby Arlen were back in the living room with us when Dr. Pinel finally emerged from the guest room.

"The boy is young and healthy," he told us. "He'll heal quickly, but I don't want him moved for the next few days. And please don't disturb him tonight. I've given him a sedative, and he should sleep until morning. I'll come back to see him then."

I walked him out to his car. He paused beside it and looked at me suspiciously. "What was the *other* favor you wanted to ask?"

I told him.

He sighed. "Having you for a friend, Pierre-Ange, is not always a comfortable relationship." But he opened his bag and gave me two capsules. "Only one at a time," he warned me sternly. "And not less than five hours apart."

I put the capsules in my pocket and went back into the house. Odile had gone inside the guest room to look at Gilbert. I asked Libby Arlen if she would make us all some strong coffee, and I went into the kitchen with her to help. When the coffee was ready she carried two of the cups into the living room. I followed with the other two, after taking a second to drop one of the capsules in the cup in my left hand.

Odile and her father were sitting together on the sofa, still a little stiff with each other, not talking. I gave her the left-hand cup.

Five minutes after we'd had our coffee Odile said she was feeling sleepy but didn't want to go to bed yet. Mulhausser stood up and let her stretch out on the sofa. A couple minutes later she was sound asleep—and nothing was likely to wake her for hours.

Then I told Mulhausser that his daughter was a heroin addict.

He regarded me with horrified disbelief. I unbuttoned Odile's long sleeves and peeled them up—to let them see all the ugly needle tracks on the insides of both her arms. That convinced Mulhausser. For a moment I thought he was going to throw up. I waited until he had himself under control. Then I told him what I had in mind.

He didn't like it. His wife took his hand in hers and told him the facts of life. "I've known a lot more junkies than you, Egon. If Odile is that badly hooked, it's the *only* hope of curing her."

He knew she was right. But he said miserably, "She'll never forgive me, if I do that to her against her will."

"You have to take that chance," I told him. "Or let her go on living on that junk. It's not a pleasant life. And it won't be a long one. But that's up to you."

After that I didn't say any more, leaving it to Libby Arlen. She talked to her husband for almost half an hour. And finally he agreed to do what he knew had to be done.

I made a long-distance call to the director of the sanitorium I knew. We'd had dealings in the past. It wouldn't be the first time they'd taken a young adult into their therapy program as a virtual prisoner—after the parents signed the necessary documents of commitment.

Mulhausser and I carried Odile to his Jaguar and drove off with her. Libby Arlen was left to mind Gilbert. In the morning she was to tell him that Odile had decided to commit herself to the sanitorium—and that she didn't want Gilbert to try seeing her again until she could come back to him fully cured. However he reacted to that, he was going to find it impossible to get in to see Odile. Nobody outside the sanitorium staff would be able to see her again until they released her.

Not nice—but, as Libby Arlen had said, it was the *only* way. Odile wasn't another André Marchine; she would never be able to kick it on her own.

The sanitorium was outside Aix-en-Provence, up above Marseilles. It took us three hours to get there. Odile was still out when we arrived—and when we left after Mulhausser had committed her.

I had Mulhausser drop me off at a hotel in Aix. I spent the rest of the night there. I'd brought two pieces of luggage with me. One was my own bag. The other was the knapsack I'd first seen when Odile carried it past me while I was having my crêpe one evening on Place Rossetti, in the Old Town of Nice.

Early in the morning I rented a car, put the two pieces of luggage in, and drove up to Paris. The drive took seven hours. By plane I could have made it in one hour.

But some things I don't have nerve for. One of them is attempting to carry three million dollars' worth of heroin through airport controls.

At five that afternoon I was sharing a glass of Beaujolais and a snack at a tiny bistro with a deserved reputation for the quality of the assorted *charcuterie* it imports from every region of France. The bistro faces the green bronze equestrian statue of King Henry IV, out of the middle of Pont-Neuf, the oldest bridge over the Seine. I was sharing the snack with Commissaire Jean-Claude Gojon, a slim, cultured man with black-rimmed glasses, expensive tailoring, and a somewhat prissy expression.

He was part of the toughest group of police detectives in France: the Brigade de Recherches et d'Intervention.

We weren't exactly friends. On occasion we had been close to being enemies. But out of those occasions we had developed a certain amount of mutually wary respect.

"You may have heard," I told him, "that Didier Sabarly was expecting a shipment of pure heroin that got hijacked somewhere en route."

Gojon gave me his bored expression. "Is there anyone in Paris who has *not* heard of that by now?"

"Three million dollars' worth," I said.

"I heard *four*," Gojon told me.

I shrugged. "Give or take—it depends on how many ways they cut it before putting it out for sale on the streets."

"True. So?"

"So, I'm prepared to make you a present of that shipment Sabarly failed to get. All of it. Or almost all. Minus about a thousand dollars' worth."

Gojon scowled at me suspiciously. "*You* are."

"Yes."

"Where did you get it?"

"I didn't. *You* found it. You can make up any story you want about where and how you managed to grab it before it could be delivered to Sabarly—as long as you leave me out of your story. It would be quite a feather in your cap."

"What?"

"An American expression. Means your superiors will be impressed with you."

"I'm not that interested in impressing my superiors," Gojon said stiffly. That, we both knew, was a lie. He smiled a little. "However, I *would* enjoy seeing the expression on the faces of certain *Stups* I know."

Les stups are narcotics officers of the Brigade des Stupéfiants. Since *they* are the cops who are supposed to snatch big drug shipments out from under the noses of gangsters, they wouldn't enjoy Gojon's having beaten them at their own speciality.

"And what," Gojon asked me softly, "do you want in exchange?"

"Two things," I told him. "First, what I said: Keep me out of it. I don't want anybody asking me questions about where *I* got all that junk. Second, I want you to spread the word. Far and wide, as they say. That this is the shipment *Sabarly* was waiting for that you've hauled in. All of it. I want everyone to hear it. Especially Sabarly."

That would remove one pressure from Odile. Once Sabarly knew the police had that shipment, his people would stop hunting for it.

The pushers he supplied would have to go without a little longer. Not much longer, probably. If Fulvio Callega didn't have another shipment on its way, some other supplier would.

Didier Sabarly wouldn't have paid for the lost shipment, since it hadn't been delivered to him. And the financial loss that represented for Fulvio Callega was now the least of what he had against Mulhausser's daughter.

"A deal?" I asked Gojon.

He nodded. "Where is it?"

I reached under our table for the knapsack and dumped it in his lap.

"Here."

After that I went and had a talk with Fritz Donhoff. He begun putting out feelers throughout the *milieu*. I flew back down to the Riviera and put out feelers of my own.

Five days later the word reached us. My worst fear was confirmed.

Fulvio Callega had put out a "forever contract" on Mulhausser's daughter.

▨ **33** ▨

AFTER FOUR DAYS OF DETAILED INVESTIGATION AND PREP-
aration I drove across the border to see Fulvio Callega.

Dolceacqua is an old Italian village straddling the Nervia
River. Half an hour from the French frontier. Fifteen minutes from the Ligurian seacoast. Twenty minutes from Fulvio Callega's villa outside Ospedaletti.

Below Dolceacqua, above the left bank of the narrow
river, was a small, rustic restaurant called the Imperia. It
was noted for the quality of its fish, and its prices were
high. Behind the restaurant was a terrace for outdoor dining
and an artificial freshwater pond stocked with trout. On
warm, sunny days like this one, when Fulvio Callega was
using his Ligurian villa, he liked to have his lunch out
there.

His favorite midday meal was grilled trout, along with
pasta, a mixed green salad lightly flavored with lemon and
olive oil, and one bottle of Tuborg beer.

Fulvio Callega had accomplished much in his forty-five
years by devoting a full day of attention to his business
affairs every day. He was accustomed to rising shortly after
dawn to do so. When dining alone he usually took an earlier lunchtime than most people.

A phone call to the Imperia would reserve a terrace table
for him at precisely eleven A.M. On these occasions the
restaurant never served anyone else out there until after he
had departed.

At a quarter past eleven on this particular morning a
brown two-door Opel pulled into the gravel parking area
in front of the Imperia. Fulvio Callega's Lincoln Continen-
tal was already parked there. Its armed chauffeur leaned
against its side, smoking a short, thin cigar. Fulvio Cal-

lega's two personal bodyguards had gone inside the restaurant with him just over ten minutes earlier.

The chauffeur flicked his cigar to the gravel and straightened up as the two men in the Opel climbed out. His experienced eyes surveyed them and found nothing to worry him.

The Opel's driver was a tall man wearing thick eyeglasses and a shabby open raincoat. He brought out a cloth and busied himself cleaning dust from his car windows. His passenger was a distinguished elderly gentleman with baggy eyes and silver hair, wearing a velvet suit the color of dark wine that was cut in a fashion long out of style. He nodded politely to the chauffeur and trudged into the restaurant.

The man in the shabby raincoat continued to polish his car windows. The chauffeur lit another cigar.

Three minutes later I drove my Peugeot into the Imperia's parking lot. The chauffeur regarded me thoughtfully as I strolled by him to the restuarant entrance, but he didn't stop smoking.

The interior of the Imperia was one large room furnished with wooden tables and chairs and a short, zinc-topped bar. One of Fulvio Callega's bodyguards stood with his back to the bar, his elbows resting on it. The elderly gentleman was seated at an inside table, leaning back sleepily in his chair, his hands resting on his lap. The restaurant's owner, a stubby man who was also its chief cook, was behind the bar pouring the glass of wine the elderly gentleman had asked for.

Through an open rear door I could see the back terrace. Fulvio Callega was out there having his lunch at a circular table beside the fish pond. The table was large enough to serve six, but he had it to himself, as was his custom. His other bodyguard sat at a separate smaller table.

I walked through the room toward the doorway to the terrace. The inside bodyguard's growl brought me to a stop. My Italian was sufficient to understand his command—and the restaurant owner's polite explanation that the terrace was not available until after noon.

The chauffeur walked in the front door, not looking happy about it. Jean-Marie Reju was walking close behind him. The chauffeur put his hands down on top of the bar. Reju rested one fist on the bar, pointing his big Colt .45 down its length.

Fritz Donhoff raised a hand from his lap, holding his Beretta 92SB pistol. He instructed the inside bodyguard and the restaurant owner in quiet, excellent Italian: "Please put your hands on the bar and then remain that way until we leave."

The restaurant owner obeyed immediately. The bodyguard was slower, but he finally forced himself to turn and face the bar, placing his hands down flat on it. Reju remained in position, his .45 covering the three men now standing with their hands on the bar. Out on the terrace Fulvio Callega and his other bodyguard continued to sit at their tables, unaware of what had just occured inside.

I walked out onto the terrace.

It took up the rest of a small hilltop occupied by the restaurant. Beyond it the land dropped into a wide, empty ravine that rose on the other side to a forested hill seven hundred yards away.

Fulvio Callega looked up at me in mild surprise. His outside bodyguard came to his feet as I started past him, his hand sliding inside his jacket toward his gun.

Fritz Donhoff stepped outside and aimed his Beretta at the side of the bodyguard's face, freezing him with his hand still out of sight under his jacket.

I spoke to Fulvio Callega in English: "Advise your man to bring his hand out in the open, empty, and sit down with both hands on the table. That old man with the pistol assassinated more Nazis during the war than any other Resistance fighter in Paris. Of course, he *is* very old now— which might tempt your man to try a fast move. It wouldn't be a good idea. For him or you."

Fulvio Callega gave his bodyguard a quiet command. The man sat down, scowling, and put his empty hands on the table.

I walked on to Fulvio Callega's big table. "My name's Sawyer," I told him. "I'm only here for a short private talk. Nothing else."

I sat down facing him. He was short and blocky in a dark, striped three-piece banker's suit, with an old-fashioned gold watch chain across its buttoned vest. In contrast with his body his face was long, with a bulging brow, a heavy chin, and a thin, taut mouth. His dark eyes held less expression than a couple of pebbles on a block of cement.

"My Italian is lousy," I said, "so let's speak English to make sure we understand each other. I hear you speak it perfectly."

Fulvio Callega nodded impassively. "I lived in the States for some years."

"And in Hong Kong for two," I added.

The dark eyes narrowed very slightly. "Not many know that."

"No," I agreed. "But I do."

"I know a bit about you, too, Mr. Sawyer. For instance, I know that somebody I once did business with has always been fond of you. Marcel Alfani."

Alfani's feeling for me usually irritated me. But there'd been times when it had been of help. I said, "That's true."

"Unfortunately, Marcel has just recently undergone a serious operation in London. And will no longer be able to give you any protection. *If* you needed any."

"He's recovering nicely," I said. "I spoke to his daughter about that yesterday, after she returned from London. He should be coming home in a couple of weeks."

"But unlikely ever to be in a condition to come out of his retirement," Fulvio Callega said. "However, you don't need his protection. Not from *me*, if that's what you came to talk about. According to Boyan Traikov, you had no part in the murder of my brother. He gave me a full account of that."

"I figured he would."

"Traikov seems to have developed an odd fondness for you, too. He says you could have killed him but didn't."

"An error of judgment," I said. "For which I don't forgive myself."

"Yes . . . it appears you are a man of heart. But a heart that does not *always* rule your head, apparently. Two other men who were after you have not been seen since."

"I came to talk to you about Odile Garnier," I said. "I don't want anyone to hurt her—any more than she's already been hurt."

"There is nothing you can do for the girl," Fulvio Callega told me flatly. "She killed my brother."

"That was a crazy thing for her to do. But Tony's the one who drove her that crazy. He turned her into an addict when she was only a kid of seventeen. Not for money or any other business reason. Just for the fun of it. He got her helplessly hooked and then tortured her with it. As a way of amusing himself."

"Tony did not always act too intelligently," Fulvio Callega admitted. "But he *was* my brother."

"He was a piece of dirt," I told him. "You never got along with him. That's one reason you had him settle in France. So he wouldn't be around to annoy you."

"In a family," Fulvio Callega said, "the blood tie is more important than any lack of affection. That girl is going to die, Mr. Sawyer. Sooner or later, someone will kill her for me. Nothing will change that—even if you have the gunmen you brought with you shoot me now. I assume you have more inside."

"I didn't bring them to shoot you, Callega. I brought them so you'll understand what kind of friends I have. I've got a lot of them, all over the world. People who can do anything that has to be done. It's important for you to understand that."

I reached across the table and picked up his beer bottle. "For example," I said, "it's not safe for this to be so close to you." I set it down in the middle of the table and leaned back in my chair.

A second later the bottle shattered. The sound from the forested hilltop seven hundred yards away reached us a fraction later. A faint snap, like a dry stick being cracked.

A single shot from a .303 Lee Enfield rifle fitted with a scope sight. One of the most effective long-range sniper's weapons there is, in the hands of an expert like Crow.

Fulvio Callega jumped slightly. He couldn't help doing that. But when he raised his eyes from the shards of splintered glass to my face again, his expression was back to impassive.

"Impressive shooting," he said calmly.

"That's what it was for," I said. "To impress you. With the fact that each of my friends has special talents. Some extremely rare."

"But it doesn't change a thing. The contract I put out on the girl is a *forever* contract."

"So I've heard."

"The money for it has already been put aside. It will be paid to whoever kills her—even if I'm dead by then. So this impressive demonstration was pointless."

"It was merely an introduction," I told him, "to what I have to say next. So you'll take it very seriously. *I've* put out a forever contract, too."

Fulvio Callega shrugged. "I've never been afraid of death."

"The contract isn't on you," I said. "It's on your son."

For the first time there was a break in his composure, quickly masked. "I have no son," he said.

"There was a woman, during your two years in Hong Kong. She bore you a son. Thirteen years ago. Your only child. You named him Francesco, after your father. Francesco Callega. That's his real name. But you've had his mother raise him as Frank Nelstrom. *Her* last name. Few people know he's yours. You've always been afraid someone with reason to hate you might retaliate against the boy."

"Who *told* you this?" Fulvio Callega was no longer impassive.

"One of the friends I told you about. You had the boy's mother move to Switzerland with him, where you go to see him now and then. As a friend of his mother, with a friend's natural interest in the boy. You send her regular amounts of money to take care of all their needs. Your son is presently attending a private boy's school outside Geneva.''

I pointed to the remains of the shattered bottle on the table. "If Odile Garnier is killed, now or in the future, certain of my friends will execute *my* contract. On your son. Even if *I'm* dead by then."

He studied me intently for almost half a minute. Then he shook his head from side to side. "No. You don't have that in you. You'd never have an innocent boy murdered."

I looked at my watch. "In a few minutes your son will come in from the school's soccer field to wash and change before having lunch in the dining room. There's something hanging on the back of the door in his room. It will be disturbed when he opens the door."

Fulvio Callega was on his feet, moving fast to the interior of the restaurant. He went past Fritz and the seated bodyguard, paying no attention at all to the gun in Fritz's hand.

I got up and walked inside after him. He turned immediately on entering and hurried through a short corridor to a phone at the end of it. I paused to scan the restaurant's interior.

Jean-Marie Reju was exactly where I'd left him, holding his .45. The other three men still stood with their hands on top of the bar. I looked down the corridor. Fulvio Callega had just finished dialing a long-distance number. No question about where: to the boy's school outside Geneva.

The connection came through, and he began speaking rapidly—in Italian. As I approached him through the corridor he stopped talking and listened. The next two words he blurted I understood: "Yes! Hurry!"

Then he waited, clutching the phone to his ear, and turned to stare at me with eyes gone wild.

"My son . . . he's already *gone* up to his room!"

His terror was too strong to leave any room for fury in his stare.

I stared back at him. Beads of sweat were popping out on his face. His breathing was audible and spasmodic. His heart must have been pounding. I hoped he wasn't about to keel over and die on me. That would render everything I'd done here useless.

A voice sounded on the line. He twisted away from me to listen, pressing one hand against the wall and leaning on it to support himself. Then he said, "Thank you"—and he hung up.

He stayed that way for a time, one hand against the wall, the other still on the phone, his back to me, waiting until his heart and lungs settled down a bit. When he turned to look at me his face was impassive again. But his voice was not quite steady yet.

"The box on the back of his door . . . a box of chocolates."

"He can eat them," I said. "They're not poisoned. But the next time, *anything* he eats could be. Or the box hanging on his door could be a bomb. There are so many ways, Callega. I *hope* you take my point. Your son is totally vulnerable, and he always will be. When he's sixteen . . . or thirty. Or your age. Any time. If Odile Garnier is killed, your son dies."

Fulvio Callega said flatly, "You *are* bluffing."

"I could be. You ready to wager the life of your only child on it?"

He fell silent, studying me again—and thinking of the terrifying minutes he'd just been through.

"Take the contract off her," I told him. "It's the only way you can be sure your son will get to live his life."

I turned away from him, walked back to the main room of the restaurant, and called to Fritz. The bodyguard out there walked in first, Fritz following him with the Beretta.

Fulvio Callega came out of the corridor. I looked at him and then signalled to Fritz and Reju. They glanced at each other uncertainly. "Go ahead," I told them.

They backed out of the restaurant, not putting away their guns until they had reached the Opel. Fulvio Callega's bodyguards and chauffeur looked at him, waiting for his word to make their moves. He motioned for them to stay as they were. I heard the Opel drive off. By now Crow was also on his way home.

I spread my empty hands and told Fulvio Callega, "If you want to call my bluff, now's your chance. It's your quickest way to find out. The contract on your son goes into operation if *I'm* killed, too."

We looked at each other some more, and then he nodded. "I'll take the contract off the girl. Nobody touches her."

I nodded back. "Then nobody will touch your boy."

I drove to the Ligurian coast and along it in the direction of France—and my pulse still wouldn't come back to normal. I finally stopped at a roadside bar and had a drink. Not wine or brandy this time. A stiff shot of whiskey. Sometimes it's the only thing.

I downed it and waited, breathing in and out. Then I raised a hand and spread the fingers. No tremble.

I got back in my car and drove home.

◈ **34** ◈

WHEN I PARKED IN MY CARPORT AND CLIMBED OUT OF THE Peugeot the first ones I saw were my mother and Arlette Alfani. They were in bathing suits, climbing a ledge path to the top of the highest cliff overlooking the sea cove below the house. I stayed rooted where I was, watching them.

They reached the top, and Babette got poised to dive first. I didn't *want* to watch. As a kid I'd watched her make that dive a couple times—and then refused to look again after that. Babette was still the best nonprofessional high diver I knew. But there were sharp rocks knifing out of the water below that cliff.

She went off perfectly, going down and into the water like an arrow, exactly halfway between the deadly rocks. I breathed again.

Babette surfaced and waved for Arlette to try it. Arlette looked all the way down and finally shook her head. She descended to a projection halfway down the cliff and dove from there.

I didn't blame her. I had *never* managed to summon up enough nerve to dive off the top of that cliff.

Arlette surfaced, and she and Babette began swimming together across the cove. I started around the side of the house and stopped again. By the toolshed there was a big pile of old roof tiles, in excellent condition. Egon Mulhausser had kept his promise.

I walked onto the patio. Fritz and Reju were sitting there at the wicker table, sipping glasses of wine. Inside the house I could hear Crow and Nathalie discussing something. I told Fritz and Reju, "It worked. Callega agreed."

"Good," Reju said, and he looked at his watch and

stood up. "I have to go now, to catch my plane back to Paris."

"If you'll wait a few minutes, I'll drive you to the airport."

"That's good of you," he said, "but I've already phoned for a cab to pick me up at the top of the driveway."

"Well, thanks for your help." I shook his hand. "And just add the cabfare to the bill you send me."

Reju looked surprised and slightly hurt. "There won't be a bill this time, Pierre-Ange. This one was for friendship. I thought you understood that."

I think my mouth dropped open. He picked up his overnight bag, gave me a shy half-smile, and walked up the drive. I stared after him, still coping with my astonishment.

The people you know best can surprise you the most.

Crow came out of the house carrying a tray of sandwiches, followed by Nathalie with a fresh bottle of wine.

"Not a bad shot," I told Crow.

"Not bad at all," he admitted.

Nathalie frowned at us. "Are you finally going to tell me what you've been up to the last couple days?"

"Target shooting," Crow told her. "We had a bet on whether I've still got that old knack with a rifle, after all these years."

"He won the bet," I told Nathalie.

She gave us a faintly exasperated look. "*Boys!* American children, still playing cowboys and Indians."

I had to agree with that. Turning to Fritz, I said, "Your man in Geneva did a good job. Thank him for me."

Fritz nodded and went on gazing glumly at the Mediterranean horizon. He hadn't said anything or smiled since I'd arrived.

I sat down beside him and asked, "Is something wrong?"

"I didn't much enjoy the way you kept referring to me as an 'old man' back there at the Imperia Restaurant," he said heavily. "That was most disrespectful. And offensive."

I sighed and told him, "I'm sorry, Fritz, I didn't mean

it. I was going on my nerves, and it just came out of me. I apologize—sincerely."

He looked at me then. After a moment he patted my hand and gave me a warm smile.

"You are forgiven, my boy."

About the Author

Marvin H. Albert was born in Philadelphia and has lived in New York, Los Angeles, London, Rome, and Paris. He currently lives on the Riviera with his wife, the French artist Xenia Klar. He has two children, Jan and David.

He has been a Merchant Marine Officer, actor and theatrical road manager, newspaperman, magazine editor, and Hollywood script writer, in addition to being the author of numerous books of fiction and non-fiction.

Several of his novels have been literary Guild choices. He has been honored with a Special Award by the Mystery Writers of America. Nine of his novels have been made into motion pictures.

GET OFF AT BABYLON is the third book in the *Stone Angel* series.

Attention Mystery and Suspense Fans

Do you want to complete your collection
of mystery and suspense stories
by some of your favorite authors?
John D. MacDonald, Helen MacInnes,
Dick Francis, Amanda Cross, Ruth
Rendell, Alistar MacLean, Erle Stanley
Gardner, Cornell Woolrich, among many
others, are included in Ballantine/
Fawcett's new Mystery Brochure.

For your FREE Mystery Brochure, fill in the
coupon below and mail it to: